A REBELLIOUS BRIDE

FENELLA J. MILLER

Boldwood

First published in 2018 as *A Soldier's Bride*. This edition published in Great Britain in 2025 by Boldwood Books Ltd.

Cover Design by Colin Thomas

Cover Images: Colin Thomas and Shutterstock

Every effort has been made to obtain the necessary permissions with reference to copyright material, both illustrative and quoted. We apologise for any omissions in this respect and will be pleased to make the appropriate acknowledgements in any future edition.

A CIP catalogue record for this book is available from the British Library.

Paperback ISBN 978-1-83678-335-0

Large Print ISBN 978-1-83678-334-3

Hardback ISBN 978-1-83678-333-6

Ebook ISBN 978-1-83678-336-7

Kindle ISBN 978-1-83678-337-4

Audio CD ISBN 978-1-83678-328-2

MP3 CD ISBN 978-1-83678-329-9

Digital audio download ISBN 978-1-83678-332-9

This book is printed on certified sustainable paper. Boldwood Books is dedicated to putting sustainability at the heart of our business. For more information please visit https://www. boldwoodbooks.com/about-us/sustainability/

Boldwood Books Ltd, 23 Bowerdean Street, London, SW6 3TN

www.boldwoodbooks.com

PART I

SPAIN

1

SPAIN, JULY

Lord Peregrine Sheldon left the tent of Major Robertson pleased with his orders. He had returned from a successful mission as an intelligence officer, the polite term for a spy, behind the enemy lines last week and had been kicking his heels since then, waiting to know what his next task was.

His orderly greeted him with a raised eyebrow. 'Where to next, my lord?'

'We're to rendezvous with a group of partisans in the mountains and together come up with a plan of attack to coincide with Wellington's intentions.'

This was somewhat vague, but he knew better than to reveal more than he needed to, even though he trusted his man implicitly. O'Reilly might be an Irishman, but he was totally loyal to the cause.

'When do we leave?'

'Immediately. I take it our gear is packed?'

O'Reilly nodded. 'It's been ready for days, so it has.'

When Perry had bought his colours, he had thought he would be in the cavalry, but because of his ability to speak both Spanish and French fluently he had immediately been transferred to the intelligence service. He had been disappointed to be denied the thrill of a battle but had soon come to love his work. He had more than enough excitement and danger and was answerable to no one whilst he was away from the army.

He would have preferred to wear his uniform and rely on the speed and stamina of his horse to gallop him out of trouble like an exploring officer – but his missions were to blend into the countryside as a wine merchant seeking new supplies and not be recognised as a member of the armed forces.

There was always activity in this large tented city of soldiers. Wellington was a brilliant commander and constantly sending out companies to harry the French who were retreating steadily towards their own country. Perry was confident they would be able to break through the fortresses, entrenchments and fortified villages between here and the French border before the winter took hold.

He left the acres of tents, the thousands of soldiers, behind without a second thought. He was, of course, out of uniform and carried no military identification in case he was captured. However, he carried maps with vineyards marked on the paper in the hope this would prove his credentials.

If a French skirmisher or scout were to see him through a spyglass they should not be alarmed or alerted to his real purpose. He did in fact stop and take note of any wine producers and also placed orders with a couple. That was why he carried so much gold. They camped in a hollow and whilst his companion prepared their food he reviewed his route.

There was no urgency to his mission, as the army was still weeks away from being battle-ready. This meant he could meander about the countryside calling in at any vineyards whilst looking out for French companies and any sign of the Spanish partisans he was to liaise with.

The heat was unbearable during the afternoon so they always pitched camp in the shade and close to water if possible. They didn't carry fodder for the horses so they must always find a place with grass for the beasts to eat.

Sultan, his black gelding, had been selected especially for his ability to thrive on poor commons. O'Reilly's horse had been purchased in Portugal and, although not especially handsome, he was sturdy and equally at home in the mountains as he was in an army camp.

* * *

The next few days were spent in similar fashion and he saw nothing untoward – no French troops at all. He avoided the villages even though they were usually friendly, no point in drawing attention to himself unless he had to.

They were slowly climbing the foothills and must be nearing their destination. It was cooler in the mountains, which was a blessing. Ten days after leaving the army O'Reilly, who had been scouting ahead, returned in a rush.

'Frenchies, a platoon of cavalry, is heading this way. They don't look none too friendly, sir, battle-hardened and nasty-looking lot, so they are.'

'Then we had better make ourselves scarce.

Thank God we have not pitched camp yet. We'll lead the horses, we can hide up there behind those rocks.'

'Go on, sir, I'll remove any sign of our being here and then follow you up, so I will.'

The gelding followed him without hesitation – another thing in the horse's favour. It was unusual to find a horse so biddable. The loose scree tumbled down behind them, making a damnable racket, and he hoped it wasn't loud enough to attract the attention of the French cavalry.

'Come along, old fellow, almost there.' He pulled the reins again and the horse obediently heaved his bulk onto the narrow shelf of rock. Perry led the animal behind the rocks and was satisfied they could not be seen from below.

There was sufficient space for the two horses and men to wait in relative comfort until it was safe to descend. Going down might be considerably more difficult than ascending, but he would trust his horse to find his own way back without breaking his neck.

There was the sudden crack of a rifle. Then the unmistakable sound of a dozen horses travelling at speed in this direction. He daren't investigate as any movement might attract attention to his position.

O'Reilly hadn't had time to join him. He sent a

fervent prayer to the Almighty, not something he often did, that his orderly had managed to get away. The French cavalry thundered past below, they were obviously in pursuit of a quarry and he knew it must be his companion they were after.

His breath hissed through his teeth. At least he knew his man hadn't been killed by the rifle shot. If fortune favoured him the Irishman might escape un-scathed and they would be able to meet up again at some point.

He remained where he was for another hour and then went to investigate. There was no trace of O'Reilly and he hoped that was a good sign. The problem now was that he had little food and nothing with which to make a camp. This had all been carried by his orderly.

He slithered down the slope and then turned and whistled. Sultan responded and somehow managed to pick his way down without mishap. The fact that there was a roving troop of French cavalry in the area meant he must move in the opposite direction. The meeting with the partisans was more important than searching for his missing companion.

After two days he was higher in the mountains and certain he was undetected. However, either

O'Reilly had been killed or captured; his man hadn't caught up with him despite the fact that he was travelling slowly.

On the third day he was searching for somewhere suitable to stop overnight and came across a small clearing with a crystal-clear stream trickling down the cliff face and lush grass growing for his horse. He had finished his rations the day before, but as long as he could continue to drink his fill he would be able to travel for another few days.

There was an opening to a cave just above where he intended to camp. He gave it a cursory glance and then ignored it. Then the hair on the back of his neck stood up. There was something moving just above him. He scarcely had time to glance up and see a mountain lion about to pounce. Sultan, who was grazing quietly just below the cave, threw up his head and bolted.

Perry screamed at him, but the horse was too terrified to listen and his panicked gallop sent him towards the edge of the ravine. He managed to grab the horse's tail but was too late to prevent the inevitable. They both fell headlong into the ravine.

* * *

Perry opened his eyes but could see nothing. Either it was the middle of the night or he had become inexplicably blind. He ached all over; there wasn't an inch of him that didn't hurt after his catastrophic fall. How could he have been so stupid? He should have checked before letting his horse graze directly below the lair of a huge cat. How long had he been here? Was it a night or day?

He raised his hand slowly and traced his fingers over his face. They came away sticky. It could only be blood. He flexed each limb in turn and although stiff and sore they functioned reasonably well. If he was blind because of his accident then he might as well be dead. In fact, a broken leg would be preferable in the circumstances.

He whistled and waited to see if his horse responded. He was pretty sure the poor beast would have perished when they had somersaulted over the cliff edge. He tried again, and again nothing. He could taste the salty, metallic tang of his own blood. If he was to have any hope of surviving he must try and stem the flow coming from his head.

After blinking he could still see nothing. His eyes could swivel but they weren't functioning. He would just have to pray it was temporary, caused by banging his head, and he would gradually regain his sight over the next few hours.

At least he had fallen into the shade and wasn't being boiled alive by the merciless sun. He pushed himself onto his elbows and regretted it. He flopped back as an excruciating pain ripped through his head. He left it for a while and then attempted to sit up a second time. Same result, only this time he cast up his accounts. Then merciful blackness enveloped him.

* * *

Sofia had completed her patrol of the region and was satisfied there were no filthy Frenchmen lurking anywhere. Papa had been an English cartographer employed by the British army but had been killed two years ago. She and Mama had been taken in by some Spanish villagers. She now considered these partisans her family and was only too happy to be included in the patrols.

As she was about to turn her horse and head back to the village, her horse shied and she lost a stirrup.

'What is it? What has disturbed you?'

She patted the animal's neck and he calmed beneath her touch. She decided to investigate. Perhaps a goat had become stuck in the ravine and needed her assistance. These animals ranged freely but still belonged to someone or other in the village and were therefore her responsibility.

She dismounted and tethered Pedro to a convenient branch. 'Wait here, boy. I shan't be long.'

Once, when she had been on a patrol in the early days, she had made the almost fatal error of not taking the correct precautions before going to investigate a suspect noise. If it hadn't been for Carlos, the French soldier would have shot her. Instead, the Frenchman had had his throat slit. It had taken her several weeks to recover from this shocking episode but now she was more resilient.

So far, she had not had to stab or shoot anyone herself – she wasn't sure she would be able to do it – but she carried a knife and a pistol and knew how to use both. She had also seen three other bodies and thought herself immune to such sights.

She pulled out the pistol from the holster attached to her saddle – she rode astride as everyone did in the mountains – cocked and primed it just in case, before making her way to the edge so she could look over and see what had scared her horse.

Her lips curved at the thought of what her grandmama, Lady Amanda Appleby, would say if she could see her now. Gently bred young ladies were expected to dress in pretty muslins, ride side-saddle, and be subservient to the gentlemen of the family. She glanced down at her man's garb: shirt, waistcoat, breeches and riding boots. Her hair was worn in a braid that hung down her back.

When the war was over and the French had been driven from Spain and Portugal, it was possible Mama would wish to return to England – but she doubted it. She rather thought she was about to have a Spanish stepfather – the leader of the small town, Carlos's father, was definitely interested in marriage.

She dropped to her knees and then peered over the edge. She almost toppled head first, so great was her shock. There was a magnificent horse lying dead at the bottom of the ravine and a few yards away was the rider – and he looked in little better case. Then she saw his hand move. He was alive and definitely not a Frenchman. Although he wasn't in uniform she recognised his clothes as coming from an English tailor.

However much she wanted to she could not get down to aid the injured man. She would have to go back and bring her comrades and some rope. She prayed the young man survived long enough to be rescued. His head was matted with blood and he was pale as a ghost beneath the gore.

It took scarcely a quarter of an hour to gallop home and her arrival attracted the attention she had hoped. She tumbled from the saddle and explained the reason for her precipitous entrance.

'We must get back there immediately. I fear the young man might have bled out before we reach him.'

Her mother handed her the haversack in which were the necessary items to deal with the injury. 'Are you quite sure he is not a Frenchman, my love?'

'I am, Mama. The ravine is not so deep I could not recognise the cut of his clothes. His horse was English too, a great shame it perished in the fall.'

Outside the men had gathered the necessary ropes. Carlos tossed her into the saddle. 'Sofia, lead the way and we shall follow.'

They travelled as speedily as she had and she pointed to the cliff edge. 'He's down there. I think it no more than seven or eight yards, so it should not be too difficult bringing him out.'

Carlos strode to the edge and looked down before answering. 'The man's still alive. As long as he has no broken bones or damage to his insides, raising him should not injure him further.'

'Lower me down first so I can attend to his head wound before you move him.'

No one argued with her suggestion and the rope was passed around her waist and knotted firmly. She then stepped off the edge and inched her way down using the rope to support her. She dropped to her knees beside the man and gently shook his shoulder.

'What is your name? We have come to help you. Try and stay awake; it will aid your recovery.'

The man groaned and his eyelids flickered then opened. For a few seconds they were unfocused then he managed a half-smile. She bent down in order to hear his whispered words.

'English girl? I had my Spanish ready.'

'I am Spanish by adoption. Keep talking to me whilst I attend to your wound.'

She couldn't clean it here – that would have to be done when she got him home. The injury ran across his forehead just above his eyebrows. It would need suturing. This was something she was adept at and would present her with no problem. She pressed a clean pad of cloth across the gash and then quickly bound it tight. Hopefully, this would stop further loss of blood.

'Can you move your limbs? Do you have any other injuries?'

'Nothing broken but I am blind. I pray that this is temporary.'

'I will know more when I have examined you and cleaned you up. It's possible your loss of sight is nothing permanent but merely caused by the force with which you hit your head.'

There was a noxious pile of vomit to one side, which indicated he had probably sustained a serious concussion. The fact that he was conscious and able to converse coherently was a good sign. Although she had sounded positive about his vision, in fact she was not so sanguine. Only time would tell if this young English gentleman would ever see again.

His eyes were the hue of cornflowers. She had no notion what colour his hair was beneath the blood. He could be fair or dark – but it was no concern of hers.

Carlos and two others landed beside her. 'He's ready to move. You must be very careful with his head as he has sustained a serious injury and further damage could be fatal.'

She stepped aside and allowed the men to gently tie the rope under the Englishman's shoulders. They were used to working together and had no need to exchange words in order to get the job done. Carlos looked up and waved and the two men remaining above disappeared.

The ropes would have been attached to one of the horses and they would be guiding it backwards. The rope tautened and slowly the patient was pulled to his feet. He was taller by a head than any of the partisans and his shoulders were broad. He was a fine figure of a man and she hoped he recovered and was able to return to his position with Wellington. That he was attached to the English army she had no doubt. Why else would he be wandering around the foothills?

Her rope also straightened and she was able to travel up beside him and keep his head from knocking against the cliff. He had passed out again, which was probably a blessing in the circumstances. Transporting him to the village was going to be difficult, but Carlos was used to returning with injured men after skirmishes with the French. Therefore, she was confident they would be able to complete this mission successfully.

They could hardly hang him across the saddle as they would a corpse or a prisoner – therefore, she would have to think of something else as she doubted he could remain in the saddle even with someone riding behind him.

The men were ahead of her and had already constructed a rudimentary sledge upon which to place him. This could then be dragged behind a horse. Fortunately, the track to the village was downhill most of the way and relatively smooth.

They had used her mount, which was sensible, as she intended to walk beside the patient. He remained comatose and she was becoming concerned for him. The sooner he was back and attended to the happier she would be.

2

PORTUGAL, SEPTEMBER

'Godspeed, your grace,' the ship's captain said and bowed.

Beau thought the man was glad to see the back of him and his charges. Beth, Miss Elizabeth Freemantle, his cousin, had proved an indifferent traveller and had spent the entire journey confined to her cabin complaining bitterly about the seasickness. Being the Duke of Silchester had given him a decent berth but not much else.

The four horses he had brought with him had also proved problematical as they had also travelled reluctantly. He had purchased these animals especially for his rescue mission to find his younger brother, Peregrine, who had been listed as missing somewhere in the no man's land between Portugal and France.

Once Beth and her long-suffering maidservant had disembarked, along with their numerous trunks and boxes, he sent his groom to hire a carriage to convey the two of them to Vitoria where she was to marry her betrothed, an officer in Wellington's army.

He had persuaded his brother-in-law, Lord Carshalton, to part with two of his employees for the duration of this visit. Jenkins and Smith were former soldiers and had served on the Peninsula and would be essential if he was to find Perry behind enemy lines. They might be long in the tooth but they were fit and exactly what he needed.

'Cousin Beau, please do not ask me to travel anywhere today. I must have at least one night on dry land to recover after that appalling experience on board ship.'

'Beth, my dear, it has already taken me far longer than I'd hoped to get here. I'm not prepared to delay any longer. Therefore, resign yourself to continuing your journey in a carriage today. We shall overnight at the first decent village we come across so will not be travelling for more than an hour or two. Surely you wish to get to young Sullivan as soon as possible?'

Mentioning the young man she was to marry was

sufficient to change her frown to a sunny smile. 'You are quite right. I cannot wait to see him and become his wife. How long do you think it will take us to travel from Oporto to this place where he is?'

'It is at least two hundred miles, so I imagine over the kind of roads we must travel it is going to take us ten days at least.'

She sighed theatrically and mopped her brow. 'Is it going to be so unpleasantly hot all the time?'

He laughed. 'My dear girl, I did warn you that it is much hotter here than it is in England, but you would insist on coming. I am sure you will become acclimatised in time. I should dispense with such elaborate gowns and wear something light and simple in future.'

He turned away as Jenkins approached on the rangy chestnut gelding. 'Your grace, Smith's found something I reckon will do nicely. He's just giving it a bit of a spruce-up before the ladies get in. He'll be along in half an hour.' The man grinned. 'Got a decent enough coachman to agree to come with us. I reckon he was eager to get away from his nagging missus.'

Beau had had the foresight to have the luggage carried to a less crowded part of the docks where they could wait in relative comfort and shade. He was holding the reins of his own mount, Sylvester, a giant black stallion, and the one he had brought over for Perry. This animal, almost as big, was a bay and went by the name of Billy. Both horses had been fed and watered once they were on dry land and now seemed comparatively calm.

'Excellent. When we are on our way, you need to ride ahead and find us somewhere to stay tonight.'

Jenkins touched his forehead politely and guided his horse in a tight circle and trotted off in the direction from which he had come.

* * *

Eventually they were on their way, trunks tied securely to the rear of the carriage, his own belongings in the saddle bags. Billy was being used as a temporary packhorse. It was damnably hot and he had not been riding for more than an hour before he discarded his topcoat. God knows how the soldiers managed, sweltering as they were in their thick serge uniforms and carrying practically their own weight in equipment.

The route they were travelling was busy with carts and the troops that had just arrived on the same ship they had. The soldiers had been disembarked first, which was only right as they were about to fight for King and Country, and so had several hours' start on them.

Despite the baking heat the men they saw marching seemed cheerful enough and stepped aside to allow them to pass when necessary. Smith was leading Billy and Jenkins rode with his friend. Neither of the men seemed inclined to speak to him unless forced to and he wasn't sure if this was because they were in awe of his title or because they didn't much care for him. Possibly they resented having been dragged away from their comfortable life with Carshalton and hadn't volunteered, as he'd been told, but been ordered to accompany him.

Whatever the reasons, it was of little importance to him. As long as they did their job, which was to guide and protect him when they started searching for Perry, he would be content. He had no wish to socialise with his servants – not a good idea for a man in his position.

The inn where Jenkins had reserved rooms for them was adequate, clean and relatively comfortable. The food was well cooked and even Beth didn't complain.

'We shall be starting at dawn, Beth, so I suggest you retire now.'

'I intend to do so. I am quite fatigued. Goodnight, Cousin, and thank you again for allowing me to travel with you.'

He smiled and she left him to his wine. It was good, a local brew but perfectly acceptable. The establishment was heaving with military personnel. The officers had eaten in a different room for which he was grateful. Beth was a lovely young lady and he had not wished to spend his time fending off unwanted advances from the gentleman concerned.

When he had heard from Horse Guards that Aubrey's twin, Perry, had failed to return after a mission behind enemy lines he had decided he would go and look for him himself. He had more resources and time than the army were prepared to spend on one missing intelligence officer.

The French were slowly being driven back towards their own country by the brilliance of Wellington. He could not imagine his younger brother was dead – he was certain he would somehow know if this was the case. Aubrey didn't even know Perry was missing as he was, as far as he knew, somewhere on the other side of the globe in the family yacht on an extended wedding trip.

Beau was well prepared for this venture. The only thing that bothered him was the fact that he'd had to bring his funds in gold and silver coin. Naturally, this had been spread amongst the saddle bags of himself, Jenkins and Smith. Hopefully, if they were attacked, at least one of them would be able to hang on to their share of the money.

He also had his pistols and the necessary paraphernalia to shoot them. Jenkins and Smith had been riflemen and they carried these weapons attached to their saddles. All three of them also had a stiletto secreted in their boot. If it came to a fight with the French army they would be vastly outnumbered and no doubt shot as spies. However, he thought they could hold their own against any riff-raff or deserter that they came across.

He spoke excellent French and passable Spanish, so he hoped he would make himself understood to any partisans he might meet in his search. He was pinning his hopes on the fact that Perry was with the partisans somewhere in the mountains and had not been able to rejoin his regiment for some reason.

He had three months at the most to find his brother before the winter set in and he was determined to do so or die in the attempt. His first task was to deliver Beth to her future husband but after that he would be free to start his investigation.

* * *

Weeks passed and Perry had still not regained his sight. Unfortunately, neither had he any notion as to who he was. The only thing he remembered was that his given name was Perry, but apart from that he could remember nothing about his past, his family, or why he was in Spain in the first place.

His hearing had sharpened as had his sense of smell, but that was no compensation for not being able to see. 'God dammit to hell!' For the third time that day he sprawled on his face after walking into something he hadn't anticipated being there.

'There's no need to swear, Perry – that is getting you nowhere.' Sofia didn't attempt to help him up as she knew that would enrage him further. She was no more than an arm's length from him. Her scent was unmistakable – something floral heavily overlaid with saddle and horse.

He surged to his feet and reached out before she could react. His hands caught hold of her shoulders and he pulled her close. 'I'm a useless lump of a thing. It would have been better if I'd perished along with my horse.'

'You are hurting me, Perry. Please let me go.'

Instantly he released her. 'I apologise, sweetheart,

but I notice you didn't disagree with my assessment of the situation. I'm a liability and an expensive one at that. I can do nothing to help the village and yet they still have to feed and clothe me.'

'Is that what's upsetting you? You had sufficient gold in your saddle bag to pay for your lodgings for a decade. The fact that you handed it over to Pablo without being asked endeared you to everyone. Because of your generosity we shall all benefit this winter.'

She took his hand and led him like a child to the paddock in which the horses and donkeys were kept during the warmer months. There was a large barn to stable them during the freezing, snow-filled winter months. Only the wealthiest owned a horse – the rest made do with a donkey for transport.

'We shall ride. That is one thing you can do as well as anyone here.'

'I find it deucedly strange that I can converse in Spanish as well as English and can ride a horse when I don't know anything else.'

'It's in God's hands. There's nothing you or I can do about it. I think it's still possible you could recover your memory. Once you do so then we will be able to send word to your family who must be desperately wondering what has happened to you. You might not be able to see, but there will be a place somewhere you can live happily.'

Perry could even tack up his horse without assistance, and he trusted the Spanish animal not to take him anywhere he didn't want to be. Marron, Spanish for brown, greeted him with a wicker. This gelding was his. It had been agreed by the village elders that some of the money he had given them had purchased it.

As long as he had Sofia riding with him he was confident he'd come to no harm. She would call out when they were approaching an obstacle or about to trot or canter and this was enough for him to remain safe in the saddle.

The only time he was truly happy was when he was away from the village, away from what he thought were pitying faces, with the girl he had come to love beside him. This love was doomed to failure as he could never ask her to be his wife. Even if he knew his true identity he could not burden her with a husband who was blind and had to be taken about the place like a child in leading strings.

'I must leave here, sweetheart. I can't remain any longer.' He pulled gently on the reins and his horse came to a standstill. He waited and she rejoined him.

'What is it? Why have you stopped?'

'Did you not hear what I said? I don't belong in your village and I am standing in the way of your happiness. I can never marry you and whilst I'm here you have been putting me first and ignoring Carlos.'

* * *

Sofia knew why he was saying this, but she was a believer in the old adage that love conquers all. She had been in love with him since the first moment he had opened his eyes all those weeks ago. Despite the fact that he was blind, he wasn't helpless. He was a strong and handsome man. Perhaps if he had not appeared so mysteriously, she might have considered Carlos as her future husband, but now that could never be.

She edged her mare close to his gelding so their knees were touching. She stretched across and took his hand. 'Why do you say that? My mother would be delighted if we made a match of it – she thinks you are a true gentleman. She has never wanted me to marry Carlos even though she intends to marry his father as soon as I am settled.'

His fingers closed over hers. Her hand looked lost in his. 'How can I marry you when I don't know who I am? Good God, I could already be leg-shackled. I could not risk it, sweetheart, however much I should like to.'

A wave of heat travelled from her toes to her crown at the thought of what she was about to say. 'Things are different here. We have no priest since Father Reynaud died two years ago, so at least one couple has decided to live as man and wife without the benefit of clergy. It could possibly have been years before the bishop was able to find a priest prepared to come here, and they did not wish to wait.

'I don't care if eventually it turns out you cannot remain here with me, that you have obligations elsewhere, I wish to share my life with you for as long as I can in the fullest way possible.' There – she'd said it. She was offering to be his mistress, something she would not even have contemplated when she left England two years ago.

She watched his expression change. His eyes might not see but they still flashed and changed colour according to his mood. His voice was gruff when he eventually answered. 'You would live with me as my wife even though I am blind and cannot take care of you as I should?'

'I love you. Do you love me?'

He raised her hand to his mouth and kissed each knuckle in turn, making her tremble inside. 'I love you more than my life. But I cannot accept your offer, my darling. You have not thought this through. There could well be children and they would be bastards. I could not do that to you or to them.'

There were tears in his eyes and hers brimmed too.

He shook his head. 'If I thought I would be remaining here, that no one is looking for me, then things might be different. I'm certain there is someone I'm close to. Sometimes at night I can almost see them. You must see, my angel, that I have to go. When Don Pablo and the men return, I shall ask them to escort me to the English army. It's possible someone there might recognise me.'

She had no option but to tell him what the village elders had decided. 'Carlos thinks you might have been a wine merchant.'

'Yes, that is possible, but for some reason I think it incorrect.'

He dropped her hand and turned his horse towards the village. For the first time he went ahead of her, trusting today to his animal's instincts to get him home safely. If he was to leave it would break her heart. If spending the night in his arms meant she would be left carrying his child then so be it. She would have something tangible to remember him by.

She would marry Carlos and become a good wife to him, even though she could never love him as she ought. Word had come from a traveller that finally their new priest was on his way to the village and should be with them before the snow. Already families were preparing for marriages and baptisms – many of them coming a year or two later than they should be. She would speak to her mama about her plans and if she was not too horrified, then she would set things in motion as soon as may be.

3

Beau and his small party arrived safely at the English camp after an arduous and unpleasant journey of almost four hundred miles. He had been carrying a special licence which he handed to Sullivan. His cousin was mercifully asleep and had not yet emerged from the stationary carriage. Once she was awake he would have no further opportunity to speak to her betrothed.

'I am assuming that you have the ceremony arranged? I fear I cannot delay more than a few hours before I continue on my journey.'

The young man, looking splendid in his dress regimentals, bowed. 'Not only do I have the service organised, your grace, there will also be a wedding breakfast held in the officers' mess.'

'Which one of the tents would that be? Also, although it is none of my concern, where will my cousin be residing?'

'I have a splendid little house in which we will both live. I also have a cook and maid to take care of everything so Beth will not have to worry about such matters.'

'Excellent. I have grave reservations about the wisdom of allowing you to marry her whilst still on active service. However, too late to repine – I'm trusting you to keep her safe. I want your word that when she is increasing you will send her home immediately.'

The lieutenant bowed. 'You have my word, your grace. In the last letter Beth and I exchanged we discussed that very point. In that situation she would like to return to Silchester Court and reside there with you until I am able to return.'

'I would have thought she would wish to live with her mother or perhaps live with your parents – but I should be delighted to have her back.'

Their conversation was brought to a dramatic halt as Beth tumbled from the carriage squealing with excitement and threw herself into Sullivan's embrace.

His cousin was led away chattering and laughing, her maid close behind, and two unfortunate soldiers ordered to stagger along with the boxes and trunks.

An officer, a major from his epaulettes, saluted and bowed. 'Your grace, it is an honour to have you here. The wedding is to take place outside the cottage in an hour from now. That will allow me ample time to give you all the information that I have about the disappearance of your brother.'

Inside the tent it was no cooler than out. Beau had expected to find it immaculate, everything in its place, but the opposite was true. The place was strewn with items, but he was relieved to see they were not of a personal nature but military-related. Maps, documents, notebooks, a compass, a spyglass, a sword and a pistol covered the small wooden table, the canvas bed, the stool, as well as a large part of the floor space.

Major Robertson was unabashed by the untidiness. He smiled and swept the papers from the bed and stool so they could sit down. 'Forgive the chaos, your grace, I don't have time for military precision and I can't let an orderly see what I have here.'

Beau perched on the stool before answering. 'One would assume, sir, that most orderlies would not have the ability to read and write, therefore your information would remain secret.'

'Unfortunately, they will all deny being literate as this could lead to extra work, but you would be surprised at how many common soldiers can decipher enough to make them dangerous. I don't suspect them of being traitors, of wishing to sell the information to the French, but they will gossip about what they know and there are always spies somewhere in a camp this large.'

'Surely leaving the papers lying around so openly would mean that one of these spies could wander in and read them for themselves?'

'Fair point, your grace. You might not have noticed, but there are four men guarding my quarters at all times of the day and night. No one comes in here apart from myself and those I invite.'

'Then I apologise for suggesting otherwise. Now, as I must leave immediately after the wedding ceremony has taken place we had better get down to business. How long has my brother been missing and what have you done to try and find him?'

'He and his orderly were expected to rendezvous with the leader of a partisan group but they never arrived. This was in July. You must understand, sir, that we could hardly go in search of them as they were behind enemy lines. We have had to rely on the information we have been able to obtain from villagers and partisans.'

'Which is?'

'Nothing at all, I'm sorry to inform you. There's been no sighting of either of their horses or themselves. It has now been more than ten weeks since they vanished and we must assume that they are either dead or prisoners of the French.'

'I thought it was customary for the names of prisoners of war to be exchanged.'

'That is true. Their names were not on the last list we received, but there is a slim possibility that they are being held by one of the roving companies who work more or less independently from their regiment.'

'Then if you would kindly show me the exact position of the proposed meeting so I can mark it on my map, I shall leave you to your work.'

'I can do better than that, your grace – I have already prepared a map and marked on it the route he might well have followed.' He handed over the paper and Beau perused it carefully.

'Thank you, this will make it easier for me to retrace his possible path.'

The major's expression was grim. 'I must tell you that

I think this mission foolhardy and highly dangerous. It is only because you have three other brothers able to take over your responsibilities if you perish that convinced Wellington to give you permission to make the search.'

'I do not require anyone's permission. I am not a member of your army, take orders from no one, and have no intention of leaving this country without my brother at my side.' He stood up, folded the map, and pushed it into his pocket. 'What I am about to say might seem at odds with my appearance, but I am convinced I would know if my brother was dead. We are a close family; my siblings are equally sure I will find him alive.'

He offered his hand and the major shook it. 'I wish you godspeed and good luck, your grace. You are going to need it.'

'There is another possible explanation for his absence. He could have been severely wounded and is unable to travel. I believe that is the most likely of the three.'

The hired carriage had already departed and the wedding party was gathering outside the house. The padre was waiting with Lieutenant Sullivan and there were a dozen or so other officers milling around. The fact that there were no other women was a worry –

Beth would need someone to guide her. Following the drum was not an easy path for any young lady and especially not one as pampered and volatile as his cousin.

He supposed he should have made more of an effort with his own appearance, but he had no time for such nonsense. Finding Perry was more important than a wedding.

* * *

Perry had been given a small house for his occupation and one of the local women and her daughter took care of the house and cooked for him. Juan, the son of the blacksmith, had become his orderly. Indeed, he had become far more than that and he considered the young man as a friend. It had been surprisingly easy adjusting to being dressed, bathed and shaved by someone else, and he could only suppose that in his past life he had had a manservant taking care of his every need.

Juan had led him around the house a couple of times until Perry was certain he could make his way without accident. Here he was confident; it was outside the problems arose.

'Perry, I have a gift for you. I think this will make

things easier for you to move about the village without falling flat on your face every five minutes.'

They conversed in Spanish, of course, but he was slowly teaching his friend to speak English as he thought it might well come in useful.

'A gift? How exciting – I am agog.'

There was something different about the smell of the house. He could hear someone else, or something else, breathing in the rear of the house where the kitchen was.

He snapped his fingers. 'Come here, boy, I wish to meet my new canine companion.' Immediately, a cold, damp nose was pushed into his outstretched hand. He fondled the dog's head and then ran his hands along his back, down his hindquarters and back to his head.

'God's teeth! You are enormous. Does he have a name?'

Juan laughed. '*Zorro de Plata*, but we call him *Zorro*.'

Silver Fox was an excellent name and it must mean the animal was grey in colour. 'Well, Zorro, are you a wolfhound or something similar?' The dog licked his hand and pressed his considerable bulk against his leg.

'He is something similar to that, a Spanish version, but he is an intelligent animal. We thought he could be your eyes.'

'Guide me? That is a novel idea, but I'm prepared to give it a go. I cannot see it working as dogs are more interested in chasing rats and rabbits than anything else.'

'Here, put this on him. I had it made especially. I have experimented and Zorro didn't allow me to fall over anything.'

Perry laughed. 'You didn't fall because you could see where you were going.'

'I kept my eyes closed...'

'This might be an intelligent animal, my friend, but I hardly think he would know the difference. However, I am delighted with my gift. I love dogs and we always had several at home.' He couldn't prevent his yell of triumph. 'My memory is coming back. That's the first thing I've remembered about my past. I had worked out that I am from a wealthy family, but only from my diction and garments. Those were deductions not memories.'

Zorro instead of running away, which one might have expected, had pressed himself tighter against Perry. 'Good boy, I think we are going to be firm friends.'

His yell had attracted the attention of those in the

square near enough to hear. They didn't knock before entering; the front door was always ajar. They asked for permission to come in and he immediately gave it.

'Is there something wrong? We heard you shout and thought you injured,' someone enquired. He recognised the voice as belonging to an elderly matron, the village gossip.

'I am perfectly well, ma'am – my shout was because I believe I am starting to recover my memory.'

'That's all very well, young man, but until you recover your sight you're less use to us than a donkey.' She stomped off muttering to herself. His initial happiness had been crushed by her casual remark. She was right. Without sight he was an unnecessary burden. Sofia had insisted the coin he had carried was more than enough to pay his way for years, but he doubted that was the case.

Juan muttered something under his breath but was careful not to say anything derogatory that could be overheard by the old lady, who was no doubt lurking outside the door at this very minute.

'Don't listen to her, my friend; we're in no hurry to get rid of you as you would insist on taking your fortune away and the don is reluctant to part with it.'

'In which case, I shall remain until you change

your mind. Shall we see how Zorro performs as my guide?'

He slipped the leather harness over the dog's head and fumbled with the buckles until he had it snugly fitted. 'Do I have this on correctly?'

'Perfect. You hold on to the loop between the animal's shoulders. Can you find it?'

'I have it. An ingenious contraption – let's hope it works. I can see only one snag in this experiment. As I have no idea where anything is how can I direct him? He can hardly decide for me.'

'I shall walk with you initially and ensure you don't come to grief. Where would you like to go first?'

'The tavern.'

Zorro remained with his shoulder pressed against Perry's thigh. 'In which direction must we go, Juan?'

'Across the square, then it's the third building on the right.'

He was pretty sure there was a well in the middle of the square, which Juan made no mention of. He was either going to go head first into it or the hound would lead him around safely. A good test to see if this bizarre scheme worked.

At first his steps were tentative, then he lengthened his stride as he became more confident. The animal changed direction and he followed his lead. Juan slapped him on the back with rather too much enthusiasm, making him stumble.

Zorro spun, snarling ferociously, and for a horrible moment he thought the dog was going to attack. 'No, boy, I don't need protecting from him.' Instantly the hackles went down and Zorro reached around and licked his hand. 'I take it we negotiated the well.'

'I truly think this is going to work. That beast understands you can't see – don't know how that can be – but he's yours now and no mistake.'

The small beerhouse, only the front room of a cottage really, served wine from their own vines, which was perfectly drinkable. It was more a place for the men to congregate than somewhere to get drunk.

He recognised most of the voices. The place was already half full, and he greeted them by name. They were impressed with his new companion but when anyone tried to fuss the dog a deep growl rumbled in his throat. Perry wasn't sure if this possessiveness was going to be an asset or a hindrance in the future.

The small town, Esposito, had more than five hundred inhabitants. The houses where he was living were stone-built and sturdy. He was familiar with the small square in which he resided but had not ventured anywhere else. Here they were self-sufficient and grew all their own food and raised livestock for milk, meat and leather. The younger men rode out to harry the French but were not totally committed to being partisans. They put family and food first.

He stayed for half an hour and then thought he would try and find the stables without assistance. Juan had abandoned him as he had business to attend to with Pablo and the other partisans. They were probably planning a final raid on the French before they were snowed in for the winter.

He stood outside and sniffed. The waft of horses definitely came from further ahead and he was certain he could hear the animals munching their hay.

'Come along, Zorro, I want to introduce you to my mount.' He had taught the horse to answer to a whistle, which had taken him some time, but he was certain the horse would come even if he whistled when he was away from the village.

He walked briskly towards the field and his canine companion loped along beside him. Perry whistled loudly and heard the gelding respond. The tack for his horse was always put in the same place and he was pretty sure he could find it without Sofia or Juan to help him.

'Now, Zorro, meet Marron. You must be the best of friends in future.' He released his hold on the dog and encouraged him to walk ahead. There was the sound of snuffling and licking so he hoped this meant that the two of them had formed a bond already.

All he had to do was keep his hand on the rail and follow it round to the small building in which the saddles and bridles were kept. The ones he needed hung on the first pegs on the left of the door. He carefully put the saddle over his arm and added the bridle.

There was a bar that had to be lifted in order to enter the field and to his delight Marron was standing waiting for him. The horse obediently put down his head and Perry slipped on the bridle and fastened the buckles. The small blanket went on next and then the saddle, which fitted snugly across the animal's withers.

'There, the girth is tight, the stirrups are down, and we are ready to go.'

With the reins hooked over his arm he led the gelding through the exit and then carefully replaced the bar. He rattled it a few times to make sure it was secure then mounted the horse. This was the first time he had attempted to go out of the village on his own. For some inexplicable reason he believed Zorro and Marron were all he needed.

Why the hound had decided immediately that he belonged with him he had no idea, but he thanked God for it. For the first time since he had been brought here injured and helpless he began to feel more like himself, more able to direct his own destiny.

He laughed out loud at his grandiose thoughts. What destiny? All he knew about himself was that he came from a good home, his clothes were well made and he spoke three languages. No – he also knew that there had been more than one dog at his house.

Zorro was so tall he could touch him with his boot, which gave him the confidence to push the gelding into a collected canter. The animal was running alongside, keeping pace, and he just had to pray his trust in the two animals wasn't misplaced. Horses wouldn't canter off the edge of a cliff... Bile flooded his mouth. His horse had done just that. Something had frightened it and it had bolted.

Frantically he reined back, his heart hammering, his hands wet with perspiration. He had no idea where he was, which direction he was facing, and had told no one he was going out on his own. What lunatic notion had convinced him he was capable of taking care of himself?

He slithered to the ground and his knees almost buckled under him. Zorro whined and pushed his nose into his hand as if encouraging him. The horse stood patiently, unbothered by the strange behaviour of its rider.

'We shall have to wait here, my boy, until they send out a search party. They will think I'm touched in the attic to have gone out on my own.'

Slowly his heart returned to normal and he was able to think logically again. A soldier didn't panic in the face of danger. A jolt of something raced through him. He had been a soldier – what the hell had he been doing out of uniform? He must be a damn spy for the English.

He slowly turned a full circle. The sun was setting and he could feel it on his left cheek – so this was the west. He had ridden directly into it. It had been on his face, so he should find his way back safely if he kept it on the back of his head. The rest he must leave to his horse and his hound.

4

Sofia had been out gathering medicinal herbs to add to her stock for the winter months. Her skills would be called upon when it was cold and the children and the old folk became unwell with chesty coughs and other seasonal ailments.

Another reason she had gone was so she could be alone, have time to consider her rash plan to seduce Perry. She had yet to broach the subject with her mama and the more she thought about it the less certain she was that her parent would agree. What was acceptable for a village girl would not be considered so for herself, who came from a prestigious family, whose grandfather had been an earl even if he had disowned her mama for marrying beneath her.

Papa was respectable, but he was not aristocracy, not grand enough. Her grandmother, Lady Amanda Appleby, had only been able to re-establish contact after the earl had passed away. Although her papa had never been welcome under her roof, Grandmama had showed an interest in herself and would have paid for her debut, had they had not been stranded in Spain.

It was quite possible her grandmother was not even aware that they were still alive, as otherwise why hadn't she sent out a search party? Sofia's lips curved at the idea. Once they had crossed into French territory they might as well have been on the other side of the world – only the foolhardiest, or most courageous, of gentlemen would venture into enemy territory.

If she had remained in England she would no doubt have married a worthy man, selected for her by her grandmother, and spent the rest of her life doing her watercolours, embroidery and taking food parcels to deserving villagers. On balance, despite the privations of her present life, she would rather be in Spain and have the freedom that she did than be cloistered and pampered in England. Just sometimes she wished she had a pretty gown to wear and a handsome gentleman to dance with at a grand party.

Her mother greeted her with enthusiasm. 'Sofia,

there has been much excitement this afternoon. Juan gave Perry a large dog in the hope that it would guide him around the place and prevent him from tripping over things.'

'I take it from your expression that it has been successful.'

'It has, my love, but even more exciting is the fact that he is starting to recover his memory. God willing, he will one day get back his sight as well.'

Sofia hoped she sounded suitably pleased but inside she was devastated. When the man she loved knew who he was he would wish to return to his family and would be lost to her. If he recovered his sight then he would continue with whatever had brought him here.

'Here are the herbs we need, Mama. Please excuse me, I wish to speak to Don Pablo.'

She hurried across the square, pausing occasionally to speak to those she met, and arrived at the large house occupied by the most important person in the town. His house was larger than all the others, and better equipped than the cottage she and her mother occupied.

He was sitting at the rear of his house, on the veranda, drinking a mug of cider. This too was produced locally and she much preferred it to the wine.

'Don Pablo, could you spare me a few moments? There is something I must ask you.'

'Come and sit with me, little one. Whatever is bothering you will not get worse because you rest for a minute. Pour yourself a drink and tell me what you have been doing these past few days, as I've scarcely seen you.'

She did as he suggested and they exchanged pleasantries for a while before she returned to the reason she had come. 'I am certain that Perry was a spy. He could only have been in this remote area if he was coming to meet someone. Have you heard from any of your compatriots if they were expecting a person to come from Wellington's army, but who failed to arrive?'

'I haven't been in contact with neighbouring groups since he arrived here. However, I have sent word with the peddlers that came through here last month. Word will get back to us eventually.' He put down his stone mug and looked closely at her. 'You do not want him to leave, do you? I see your eyes light up when you look at him – you never look at my son in this way. You must not marry Carlos out of duty, little one; you must follow your heart.'

She choked on her cider and by the time she had finished spluttering and coughing they were joined by his wife and two daughters who had come to see what all the fuss was about.

'Thank you for the drink, Don Pablo, and for your wise words.'

The sun was setting. It did so quickly here and would be dark shortly. She had still not decided if she would go through with her outrageous scheme. Perhaps if she spoke to Perry, congratulated him on his new companion, she would have a clearer view of the way forward.

She saw Juan outside the house. 'Is Perry in? I wish to see his hound. Everyone is talking of nothing else.'

'I've no idea where he is. He went towards the horses an hour ago. I was about to go and look for him.'

'I'll go.'

* * *

Perry gave the horse his head and attempted to relax in the saddle and trust his safety to his two companions. Marron whickered, increased his pace to a brisk canter, and he was finally able to breathe normally. His keen hearing picked up the sounds of the town. He was back without mishap.

It took him longer to remove the saddle and bridle than it usually did, as his hands were shaking. He lifted the bar, the gelding trotted through and Perry dropped the wooden pole back. 'There, mission accomplished. Come along, Zorro, I need a drink and I expect you do too.' There was a stream that ran through the meadow and more than enough grass to feed his horse, so it was only the dog he had to take care of.

'Perry, I've come to meet your friend. I'm surprised I've not seen him about the place before. He is certainly memorable. Where did he come from?'

Sofia was at his side, fussing and fondling the animal who was quivering with pleasure, and his long tail was slapping against his leg. 'I didn't think to ask. Juan gave him to me – shall we go and ask him together? Zorro, take me home.'

The beast ignored his command, as he was enjoying the attention he was getting from her. He repeated the command more sharply and this time the animal reacted. His head came up and his tail dropped and he set off in what Perry hoped was the right direction.

'I assume we are heading towards my home,' he said to Sofia.

'Not only that, he has ensured you do not walk

into the well as you did this morning. That animal is quite remarkable. Did you introduce him to your horse?'

'Actually, I went out on Marron for an hour. Don't look so horrified, sweetheart. I was perfectly safe. You know what this means?'

'Then you are more likely to kill yourself sooner than later?'

He chuckled. 'That, of course, is perfectly possible. However, it means I am now more independent, will be less of a burden to you and everyone else here. Did Juan tell you I have recalled one or two details of my previous existence?'

'My mother told me. It's the talk of the square. I'm delighted for you. I pray that your sight will also return soon.'

He slung his arm around her shoulders. 'As do I. If you are as beautiful as I think, then I cannot wait to see you for myself. I have been wondering, what kind of fellow am I?'

'You have hair the colour of ripe corn, deep blue eyes and, if it wasn't for the scar running across your forehead, you would be a prodigiously handsome gentleman.' Her tone was teasing and he loved her for it.

'And you? Describe yourself.'

'I am taller than most young ladies. I am suffi-ciently rounded to distinguish me from a boy. I have dark hair and my eyes are a mixture of green and brown.'

'As I thought, quite beautiful. Did you know that you smell mostly of flowers?'

'And what else, pray?'

'Horses and saddle soap.'

She poked him sharply in the ribs with her elbow. 'That was most ungallant of you, sir. I am mortally offended.'

They were still laughing when they arrived at his modest home. Juan had overheard their banter and joined in the merriment. When they asked him where he had discovered Zorro he didn't answer straight away.

'Tell me, why the hesitation? Did you steal him?'

'Not really, but the person I bought him from might not have been his true owner. I didn't enquire too closely.'

'As long as money exchanged hands I am satisfied the dog belongs to me. I am hungry; something smells appetising. First, I wish to feed Zorro. Do we have anything suitable in the kitchen?'

'There's no need to feed him. He catches his own dinner. Take off his harness and he will go in search of it. He'll not run away. He's yours now whether you want him or not.'

Perry turned to speak to Sofia but she was no longer there. She had slipped away without saying farewell and this was unlike her. Something was wrong and he was determined to discover what it was.

* * *

Juan ate with him and then returned to his own home, which he shared with half a dozen siblings, grandparents and parents. He supposed he should invite the young man to take one of the spare bedrooms, but he liked his privacy. The house was too small to share with anyone, even someone he liked as much as he did this young man.

Zorro was still out when Perry was ready to retire. He didn't know the exact time, but he was pretty sure it must be after midnight as the village was quiet. He had left the back door and gate unlatched so the dog could come in when he returned. Fortunately, the privy was only three steps from the kitchen door; the earth closet was in the lean-to next to the scullery and he could find his way there and back without danger of falling over.

A veranda ran along the back of the house, as it

did for all the others in this row, and could be accessed through a door in the sitting room, which was the length of the building.

He used the scullery as a washroom. It made things simpler for him. There was always clean water in a jug and a pottery basin standing close by. He stripped naked and washed himself from top to toe. Pity there wasn't a lake nearby he could swim in... Good God! That was something else he could do that he hadn't known about until today.

He groped on the floor and collected his clothes so he could take them up with him, then reconsidered. He would leave them out to be laundered and put on something fresh in the morning. With his boots in his hand and not a stitch on, he walked through the kitchen and into the main part of the house. The ground floor consisted of a dining room and drawing room – if one could designate it with so grand a name. The flagstones in the hallway were cold beneath his feet as he headed for the stairs.

As he approached them he froze. Someone was pushing open the front door. Was it the true owner of the hound come to reclaim him?

* * *

Sofia decided that it would be better if she didn't speak to her mother about her plans for the night. Only if she found herself to be increasing would it be necessary to mention her misbehaviour. Perry was getting back his memory; shortly he would know who he was and be able to send word to his family. Then he would return to his previous life and forget he ever knew her.

She was determined to create memories that would carry her through the rest of her life tied to a man she was fond of and respected but could never love. Her night-time ablutions were more thorough than usual – his mention that she smelt of horse had rankled and she was determined she would smell only of flowers when she went to him.

Once she was clean she was faced with a dilemma. Normally she wore breeches and boots like the men but she could see removing them might be awkward. Then she smiled at her silliness – it didn't matter what she wore as he couldn't actually see her. There was no need for her to be embarrassed in the slightest.

Also, if she happened to be seen in the square in anything but her usual garments this would give rise to speculation. So, unglamorous though they might be, a clean shirt, waistcoat and breeches would be what she wore. Her boots were loose-fitting as she had lost weight since she had been living in the village, which would make removing them easier.

She snuffed her candle and stretched out on the bed, waiting for her mother to be sound asleep. Mama, once in the land of nod, was impossible to wake. There was little chance she would hear her daughter leave the house or return later.

The other problem she had to overcome was that of the dog who would probably bark when she went into the house. This would rouse the neighbours and give Perry time to collect his thoughts and send her away. Then to her delight she saw the animal vanish into the olive grove when darkness fell. With luck he wouldn't return until dawn. It was impossible to tell if Perry had retired as he didn't use candles. His house was always dark unless he was entertaining.

Perry had been celibate since his arrival and from what she had gleaned from eavesdropping on the married women, a gentleman who had not lain with a woman for some time was more easily seduced. She crept downstairs and slipped out of the back door. It was a full moon, bright enough for her to see her way across the square. She was tempted to enter via the back door but didn't wish to trip over anything. The route to his bedroom would be simpler if she entered through the front.

Doors in the village were rarely locked and she prayed this was the case tonight. Gently she lifted the latch and began to ease the door open. Moonlight flooded in and to her shock Perry was standing no more than a yard from her. This would not have been a problem if he had not been as naked as a jaybird.

Her eyes widened. She had never seen anything so magnificent. This made things so much easier. Without hesitation she stepped in and closed the door firmly behind her. She heard his sharp intake of breath. He knew she was there.

They were in complete darkness, which was a blessing as seeing him the way he was had made her hot all over.

'I can think of only one reason you are here, darling girl, and I give you fair warning that if you don't turn tail and run this minute it will be too late. I might be blind, but my other senses are aroused.'

'I wish to spend the night with you before you go. I shall marry Carlos. He will take me even if I am carrying your child, so you have no need to worry on that score.'

He moved so fast she had little time to react. His arms encircled her and crushed her to him. His heat burnt through the thin stuff of her shirt. Almost roughly he caught her braid and pulled her head back so he could plunder her mouth.

She was dizzy with excitement, pressed herself closer, knew she had made the right decision. Then there was a gust of fresh air and she was sitting on her backside in the dirt outside his house. She heard the bolt slam across, making it impossible for her to return unless she went around to the back. This would mean a long trek in the dark.

One could only enter the courtyard at the back of his house via a narrow passageway and then through a small gate in the stone wall that ran along the rear of all the houses on that side of the square. These pretty areas were filled with orange and lemon trees, pots of flowers and had a veranda upon which the occupier could sit and enjoy the evening breeze.

After brushing down her breeches she scrambled up, unsure whether to return home or try again. He wouldn't expect her to be so bold as to attempt a second entry after he had so rudely ejected her. In future he would certainly lock both doors so this was her only chance.

As she entered the narrow alleyway she saw that Zorro was ahead of her. She increased her pace, slipping and stumbling in the darkness but the beast had vanished by the time she arrived. She pushed open the gate and found herself face to face with a solid obstacle.

'What a determined young lady you are, to be sure. I thought I made it plain just now that I do not intend to seduce you...'

'It is I who wish to seduce you – there can be no objection to that as I am the instigator of this assignation.'

He was still without clothing. Tentatively she reached out and rested her hand on his chest, wanting to touch his skin, if only the once. There was a sprinkling of coarse hair in the centre, which intrigued her. Her other hand joined the first and began an intimate exploration of his chest. He wasn't soft like her, but hard. He was holding his breath.

'God dammit to hell! There's only so much a man can take.' He picked her up, kicked the gate shut and strode through the house as if he had perfect vision. He bounded up the stairs and shouldered his way into a bedchamber. Too late to change her mind. He had warned her and she had ignored his words. She should be frightened; she had heard the first time could be painful, but instead she was as eager as he to make love.

5

Perry thought that if this was his last day on earth he could die a happy man. He propped his head on his elbow and listened to Sofia's soft breathing beside him. He'd never have made love to her if he thought his previous concerns that he might already be married were still valid. From today he would make no further effort to find out who he was and even if he did recover his memory he had no intention of leaving the woman he loved to distraction.

As far as he was concerned she was his wife; he didn't give a damn for the legalities, for what others might say. When the priest took up his position, he would join the queue of other couples and say his vows. The fact that he didn't know his name might present a problem if he was living in England – but here nobody cared about such things. They judged you on what they could see and not your bloodline.

The shutters rattled as a gust of wind hit them. This was followed by the patter of rain. He had been going to gently awake his sleeping beauty and then escort her back to her house. They would both be drenched if they did so now, so they might as well remain where they were in the comfort of his bed.

He didn't need to be able to see to know she was the most beautiful girl in the world. He entangled his hand in her hair. It was long, silky and had the scent of lemons. He sighed with pleasure. Thank the good Lord he had not tumbled into bed unwashed as he frequently did.

His lips curved as he relived her arrival. Would she still have continued with her plan if he hadn't been naked? He'd better get some sleep. It would be dawn in an hour or two and they must both be dressed to see her mother and explain the situation before she realised her daughter had been elsewhere all night.

As he was drifting off to sleep a series of vivid images filled his head. The first was of a young man who fitted his own description exactly, yet somehow Perry knew it wasn't himself he was looking at. Then a tall,

dark, older man smiled at him. He too looked familiar. Then a kaleidoscope of pictures of girls, large
houses, and horses flashed through his head.

These were his family. He didn't try to hang on to
the visions but allowed himself to drift further into
his dream. He heard a voice saying, *Lieutenant, Lord
Peregrine Sheldon, to see you, sir.*

He sat up so abruptly he woke his partner. 'What
is it? Do I have to leave now?'

'No, my darling, you will remain with me until
morning. Have I told you how much I love you?'

She snuggled closer and kissed his shoulder.
'Many times, my love, but actions speak louder than
words.'

Perry forgot what had woken him and, a considerable time later, finally was able to sleep. He was
roused by Zorro barking furiously.

He tumbled out of bed and dragged on his
breeches and boots. 'We have overslept, sweetheart,
Señora Rodriquez and her daughter are trying to get
in to make my breakfast. I intended that you would
have returned home before this.'

He could hear her quickly dressing on the other
side of the bed. 'Are you ashamed of me?' The tone was
light, but he detected a slight hesitation in her voice.

'You are my wife as far as I'm concerned, and we shall have the matter legitimised when your priest arrives at the village. I know for a certainty that I have never been married so am free to wed you as soon as I can.' The animal was still making a racket to wake the dead.

'I'll go down and calm Zorro – he needs to understand I shall be living here in future and he must also obey me.'

She was gone before he could protest. He moved to the door to overhear what was being said in the kitchen and he laughed. The señora was more concerned about the dog than the presence of Sofia in the house.

He cursed as he fumbled for his stockings and pulled on his spare shirt. Where the devil were his boots? Then he remembered he had tossed them aside last night and they would be somewhere in the courtyard.

Sofia let the dog out and then her light footsteps echoed on the stairs. 'Here are your boots, Perry. Do you need assistance putting them on?'

'Absolutely not. I'm glad it's stopped raining and that the sun is out.'

His words hung between them as they both understood the significance. His vision was beginning to return.

She flung herself into his arms and he kissed her fiercely and almost gave in to the temptation to tumble her back between the sheets.

'What can you see? I can't believe you might be regaining your sight.'

He blinked a few times and turned his head back and forth. 'I can distinguish light from dark, but little else.' He paused, wondering if he should tell her that he now knew who he was. Then she spoke again.

'You don't have to marry me, you know. I told you last night...'

'If you say that again I shall not be responsible for my actions. We are getting married and you will then be Lady Sheldon. I have several siblings and am convinced I have a twin.'

She became rigid in his arms and stepped away from him. 'My lord, I am delighted you have recovered your identity. I shall not marry you. I would never be accepted in your family after the life I have lived out here. My family was on the periphery of society, but I am well aware I am so far beyond the pale even marriage to you could not make me acceptable.'

'That's nonsense, and you know it. You are marrying me. Now, do you wish to breakfast here or shall we go immediately and give your mother the good news?'

* * *

Beau left the army late afternoon, determined to travel as far as possible before being obliged to make camp. Smith was leading the packhorse and Jenkins scouted ahead to make sure they were not going to come face to face with a roving French company or any other danger. There were brigands and rogues, as well as both French and English deserters, roaming this land. He was at more risk from attack from these than he was from the French.

The partisans, fighters of a guerrilla war, would hopefully be less likely to murder him. The local population hated the French. These invaders took their food and horses without payment and tortured and killed indiscriminately those who were suspected of helping the English or the Spanish resistance in any way.

Wellington insisted that his men paid for what they took and only stole from the enemy. This meant that they were tolerated, sometimes applauded, but not detested. England had previously been at war with Spain for years, disliked the Catholic Church, and it seemed strange to now be allies with previous enemies. He supposed Spain and England were united in their hatred of France, which would be enough for the moment.

Jenkins cantered back to join them. 'There's a clearing a mile ahead, your grace, off the main route, with fresh water and grass. I don't reckon we'll find anything better tonight.'

'In which case, make camp there. Will it be safe to light a fire?'

'It'll be safe enough today. No Frenchies would be stupid enough to come so close to the English army. Tomorrow it'll be different.'

The weather was clement during the day but the temperature fell rapidly at night now it was September. Sleeping under the stars was a novel experience for him but one he was coming to enjoy. As long as he found his brother and was able to bring him home again he would never regret this expedition. He had not journeyed in so remote a place before, although he had visited Italy, Greece and France when he had been little more than a green boy travelling with his tutor to broaden his mind.

He was deeply asleep when Jenkins hissed in his ear, 'It ain't safe to stay here, your grace; there's a troop coming. Smith was keeping watch and saw them no more than a mile away.'

Beau was well aware that the slightest sound travelled miles in the dark. There was a full moon, but it was obscured by cloud, which must make travelling hazardous. The fact that the French company was doing so meant they must be on urgent business – he prayed it wasn't him they were hunting.

In a matter of minutes they were mounted. 'Down here – it's going to be safer where we can't be seen.'

He urged his stallion to follow Jenkins and the spare mount, thanking God that his men had had the sense to douse the fire once they had eaten. Even if the smoke wasn't seen, the smell would have drifted to the road and revealed their presence.

The horses slithered down the slope until it became too steep to remain in the saddle. On foot he led Sylvester the remainder of the way and was breathing heavily by the time they found safety in a copse of trees.

'Here, I'll take the beasts, your grace. Best they can't see or hear the soldiers as they might call out to their horses.' Smith vanished into the darkness with the four animals, leaving him with Jenkins.

'I'd like to see who goes past. Will we be safe if we climb that tree?'

'I reckon if we stay flat behind the trunks we'll be safe enough. For Gawd's sake, sir, don't let them see your face. It'll shine like a beacon in the dark.'

They had only been in place for a few minutes when they heard in the distance the sound of horses approaching, the jangle of bits, the clank of metal-shod hooves as they hit the stones, but strangely no voices or human sounds.

He held his breath, didn't dare to put his spyglass to his eye in case the flash of the glass was visible to those above. Then the clouds cleared and the track was silvered by moonlight. A single horse jogged into sight. The cavalry officer was definitely French – that much was obvious from his uniform. The scout vanished from sight and then the road was filled with his compatriots.

There were not as many as he'd expected, possibly no more than twenty, but enough to kill or capture his small party if they discovered them. The officer in charge rode at the head of the band. It was obvious he was the senior member of the company from the ostentatious amount of silver that adorned his uniform.

The hair on the back of his neck stood up as he saw why they were taking the risk of travelling at night. In the centre of the group were two pack animals each carrying two small wooden chests. They were transporting gold and did not wish to be ambushed by the partisans.

He climbed down the tree, making sure not to alert the passing soldiers. Jenkins followed suit. Once they were safely out of earshot he gave his orders.

'Smith, you are the better horseman, gallop back to the camp and tell them what we've seen. Jenkins and I will follow the French. They will hole up somewhere during the day, which should make them an easy target.'

They didn't argue. This wasn't because he was a duke, or that he was their paymaster; it was because they were ex-soldiers and knew what he said made perfect sense. By capturing the French gold, the English could make life difficult for the enemy who would be waiting for the money in order to pay their men. Sullen soldiers didn't fight well. Without being requested to do so he took over the task of leading the horse they had brought with them for his brother.

* * *

Sofia was glowing all over. Until today she had not known what true happiness was. Of course she wanted to marry Perry, but had tried to dissuade him for his own sake, not hers. He said they would remain in Spain, but she doubted that would be the case. His family would want him home and eventually this simple life would pall and he would wish to be living in his own environment.

They had been so late getting up the village was astir, and they would be seen returning to her house together. Even Mama would be down and wondering where her daughter was. He was pulling on his boots with as much precision as a man who could see perfectly well.

'Do I pass muster? Should I shave before we go? After all, I am suddenly elevated to the aristocracy and have no wish to let the side down.' His smile made her toes curl.

'You, my lord, are a ninny. We have been looking at you for the past ten weeks and care less about your appearance than you apparently do. Hurry up, or I shall go without you.'

'I heard you let the dog out – I need to wait for him to return as I want to make sure he knows he must be at my side whenever I am out of the house.'

'You won't need him very soon, as you will be able to see again. I'm confident that as your memory returns so will your eyesight.'

They clattered down the stairs together. He called a cheery good morning to the women working in the rear of the house and unbolted the front door. Now the moment had come to exit she was reluctant to do so. It was all very well saying that she didn't care what folk thought, but she did.

'I should have told Carlos before I came. He will be devastated that I have chosen you when up until your arrival I had had every intention of eventually becoming his wife. In fact, if the priest had come before you did then I would already be married to him.'

'Then thank God he didn't. Don't dither in the doorway, my love; I wish to speak to your mother and make this betrothal official.'

He bundled her out of the door and closed it firmly behind them. Then he put his arm around her waist, making his claim very clear to the two women fetching water from the well in the centre of the square. Señora Rodriquez might have shown no disapproval, but these two had pursed their lips and she heard them muttering. She was certain they had called her wanton and little better than a light-skirt.

His arm tightened. 'Ignore them, darling. Their opinion is irrelevant.'

Her face was burning, her joy vanishing with every step she took. She had been foolish to think she could behave in such a scandalous manner, tear her precious reputation to shreds, and still walk proudly around the village as if nothing had happened.

The door opened before they reached it, but her mother had retreated to the parlour and was waiting there for them.

'Let me speak to her first. I don't want you to be given a bear-garden jaw for something that wasn't your fault.'

They were now safely inside. 'I came to you; you sent me away but I returned. How could it possibly be anyone's fault but my own?'

'You were an innocent; I am a gentleman. I should have had the strength of character to insist you left and waited until we were married before taking you to my bed.'

She stretched up and kissed him. 'Fiddlesticks to that! I don't regret what happened for a minute. I love you and I know that you return my feelings. Whatever we've heard, it could possibly be years before the priest comes – would you have been prepared to wait that long?'

'I would have preferred it if you had, Sofia, but one cannot unbreak an egg. However, I am mortified that you did not return more discreetly.' Her mother spoke from behind them. 'Perry, I think we need to talk. Daughter, make yourself useful and prepare breakfast.'

'No, darling, I'll not have you sent away as if you are of no account. Madam, I have no wish to converse in the passageway. Shall we repair to the parlour?'

She had never heard him speak so authoritatively. Somehow, knowing that he was an aristocrat had made him more formidable. A flicker of unease ran through her. She had committed the rest of her life to this man and yet she didn't know his true character at all. Had she made a catastrophic error?

'I would prefer it if you spoke to my mother alone.' She stepped away from him and walked away to do her morning chores as usual, as if her life wasn't changed forever.

Perry didn't speak for a minute, just stood ramrod straight, every inch an aristocrat until the poor woman crumpled beneath his stare.

'I am Lord Peregrine Sheldon; my brother is the Duke of Silchester. I am betrothed to Sofia and we shall be wed as soon as the wretched priest arrives. I hope this meets with your full approval.'

She curtsied and a wave of shame washed over him. He was behaving appallingly. Mrs Appleby had shown nothing but kindness since he arrived – this was no way to repay her.

He bowed formally. 'I most sincerely beg your pardon, ma'am, for speaking to you so rudely. Might I be permitted to sit?'

'Of course, my lord...'

'No, I am Perry to you and always will be.' He smiled warmly. 'I hope you will allow me to call you mama as soon as the knot is tied.'

'I should be honoured. What possessed you to march across the square so boldly announcing to everyone that you have debauched my daughter?'

He bit back an angry retort. 'You are right, ma'am, but the matter was taken from my hands as Señora Rodriquez, an inveterate gossip, arrived before we were ready to leave. It was badly done of me. We should have waited until we were married before sharing a bed.'

For the first time she relaxed and returned his smile. 'As my daughter came to you I can hardly blame you. She is a beautiful young lady but, I am sorry to say, since we have been living here she has been riding out with partisans and has become wild and unruly.'

'And I love her for it. I owe her my life and will forever be grateful that my accident brought us together.' He could hear crockery clattering at the rear of the house. Sofia was making sure neither of them forgot about her. 'I am an intelligence officer. I was on my way to a meeting. There is little point in me attempting to complete my journey as matters will have moved on by now.' He supposed he should really have told her he was a wine merchant looking for new supplies but the time for prevarication had gone. She was to be his mother-in-law and there must be complete honesty between them in future.

'I thought as much. You will wish to return to the English army I suppose. The men left last night and should be able to supply you with the whereabouts of Wellington when they return. It will be a great shock to everyone to discover your true identity.'

'I was not travelling alone. My first task is to find my companion. I think he might have been captured. I pray he wasn't shot as a spy if they caught him.'

The door slammed back and Sofia stood there glaring at him. 'I could not help but overhear what you said. Have you completely lost your senses? It has been many weeks since you were separated from your comrade. What makes you think you can find him after all this time without getting captured or killed yourself?'

'Why don't you come in, my love? One never hears good news if one is listening outside doors.'

She was holding a large skillet in her hand and for a moment he thought she might throw it at him. Then wisely she thought better of it. 'Please, Perry, don't go.

It is far too dangerous. At least wait until we are married.'

He couldn't prevent his laughter. 'If I didn't know you better, sweetheart, I would think you had an avaricious motive for suggesting that. Or is it that you just wish to be elevated to the aristocracy and inherit my fortune on my demise?' These remarks had been said in jest but were taken as truth.

Her expression changed. She raked him from top to toe with a disdainful glare. 'I don't give a fig for your money or your title. I was just thinking that if I'm carrying your child you might prefer it not to be a bastard.' Her arm swung back. She was going to throw the pan at him.

He was on his feet and at her side before she was able to do so. 'Throwing things at me...' He couldn't finish the sentence. His knees buckled and only her quick thinking stopped him from collapsing on the floor. Until that moment he hadn't taken in the fact that he could now see – not perfectly – but he was no longer blind.

Between them they manoeuvred him onto the sofa and she sat next to him, holding his hands in hers.

'When did your vision clear? How long have you been able to see me?'

He rested his clammy forehead against her shoulder and took several steadying breaths before he was able to speak coherently. 'I'm not sure exactly. I think it has been clearing since we got up but I was so full of my own importance this miracle passed unnoticed.' He pushed himself upright in order to see her clearly for the first time.

'You are even more lovely than I imagined, sweetheart. My brothers and sisters will love you as much as I do.'

'I hope them loving me was not dependent on the fact that I was pretty.' Her eyes were sparkling. He had never seen anything so beautiful.

'Strangely enough all my family have married partners that are equally as personable as they are. My twin, Aubrey, was married in the summer but unfortunately, I could not be there. Now we are to be married and I shall have none of my family present.'

'Then we should postpone our nuptials until you can return to England.'

'We shall do no such thing. I am a serving soldier, albeit an intelligence officer rather than a fighting one, but I cannot resign my commission until the war is over. I shall no longer act as a spy, but return to my company and fight alongside them when necessary.'

'Then I shall follow the drum. I think I will enjoy being a soldier's bride.'

He picked her up and put her securely on his lap. 'I must discover what happened to O'Reilly. It is my duty as an officer not to abandon him.'

'I do understand, and I apologise for almost throwing...' She stopped and looked around in bewilderment. 'Where is the wretched thing? In fact, where is my mama?'

'She will have taken it out of harm's way and left us to celebrate together. I can hardly credit that my memory and sight have returned so suddenly. One would have thought there would have been some signs before yesterday.'

'We shall put it down to the hand of God, and thank him for it.' She scrambled off his lap. 'If you are going in search of your compatriot then I shall come with you. I know these hills; I am able to use a pistol and a knife if necessary.'

He was about to tell her in no uncertain terms to do nothing of the kind but then reconsidered. 'Very well, you may accompany me.' He fixed her with the stare he used on his subordinates. 'You will be under my command and follow my orders to the letter. Is that understood?'

She giggled and saluted – well, made a passable

attempt at one. 'Yes, sir. Breakfast should be ready by now and I am sharp-set.' She paused as the most hideous noise interrupted them. 'What on earth is that?'

'I think it's Zorro announcing his return. Would your mother object if I let him in?'

'As long as he stops howling she won't care where he goes.'

* * *

Both Perry and her mother refused to allow Sofia to spend another night across the square. 'I can't see that it makes any difference. I am a fallen woman and my reputation is non-existent. Isn't this like closing the stable door after the horse has bolted?'

Her future husband exchanged a knowing look with her parent before answering. 'I should never have allowed you to stay in the first place – I shall not make the same mistake again. Another thing, do you have any gowns you might wear? I had not understood just how unseemly breeches and boots are for a young lady.'

She poked her tongue out at him and he laughed. 'I shall have a rummage about in my closet and see what I might find, but I am not promising anything. I shall wear a dress for our wedding ceremony. I insist that you have something new as well.'

'God knows where I shall find garments that fit me in this town. Now I can see I shall venture around the place and look for a tailor. I shall have to purchase everything on credit.'

'You have not visited the marketplace, the church, or any of the shops. Your knowledge of this place has been limited by your disability. We have everything we need here, and what we don't we buy from the next town.'

'Now that they know they have an aristocrat in their midst I can assure you they will be only too happy to sell you things with or without payment.'

'I must go. I thank you for the delicious breakfast, ma'am, and would like you both to dine with me tonight.'

'Thank you, that would be delightful. Sofia will be dressed appropriately for the occasion.'

Sofia followed him to the front door but was pushed aside by the dog when she tried to embrace him. 'I can see how it's going to be in future. Zorro is a jealous guardian. Shall we be taking him back with us to England when we eventually go?'

'More to the point, sweetheart, is whether I shall

be allowed to keep him when I'm back with my regiment.'

'He will have to make do with me when you are busy fighting for King and Country.' She embraced the dog and he licked her face, which was not a pleasant experience. 'Enough of that. I've no wish to be slobbered over by an animal who has just been eating raw rabbit for his breakfast.'

The dog wasn't wearing the harness and she wondered if he was aware that his master could now see and didn't need to be led about the place. Perry cupped her face and kissed her hard and she regretted the fact that they were not to spend another night together until they were married.

She opened the front door and he marched away, his dog prancing about him yelping and barking in excitement. The animal obviously understood Perry was no longer blind, which was a miracle in itself. Having Zorro for company when her husband was on active service would be both a comfort and an entertainment.

She decided to remain indoors and avoid the speculative and disapproving looks she would encounter if she went out. For all her bravado, she too regretted her impulsive decision to seduce Perry.

Everything was happening so quickly. Three days ago he didn't know who he was and had been blind – now he was a lord and could see and she was no longer an innocent.

Dinner wasn't eaten as early as in England, for here nobody sat down until late. This gave her ample time to find something suitable to wear, press it, and also wash her hair. She had been careless of her appearance when he couldn't see her; now everything was different.

'Mama, upon what have we been living these past months? I cannot believe that Papa's funds and the money you have earned from your sewing have been sufficient.'

'People are generous here, unlike at home. You treat their ailments for nothing and you might not have been aware of it but they repay this kindness with gifts of food and fuel. Also, the fact that you have accompanied them several times when they have been on raids has made you one of them. Nobody goes hungry here whilst there is food to be had.'

'Mama, will you marry Don Pablo when I leave?'

'I will indeed. We might not be giddy and heedless like you and Perry, but nevertheless we are still deeply attached to each other. I shall have position in the town married to him, and will live in comfort, if not luxury. I shall miss you dreadfully of course, but when this dreadful war is over perhaps I shall be able to make an extended stay with you in England.'

'I shall write to my grandmother telling her I am about to be married to the brother of the Duke of Silchester. That should make her happy.'

'You will do no such thing, my girl. If you intend to leave with Perry even if you are not married, it's best not to tell her anything.'

'I shall be guided by you, Mama. I'm going to find something to wear tonight. It is so long since I have worn a gown, but I am not sure I have anything the moths haven't eaten.'

'Come with me, my love. I have something to show you upstairs.'

Intrigued she followed her parent and was quite overwhelmed by what she was shown. 'How could you possibly know I would be requiring feminine apparel? When did you sew these gowns for me?'

'I thought at once how it would be with you and Perry so have been working on them for an hour or two every day. Which one will you wear tonight?'

'Where did you get this lovely material?' She ran the fine green cotton through her fingers. 'This will complement my eyes to perfection. I must hope he will not notice my lack of stockings.'

'Don Pablo gave me a box filled with cottons, silks and satins. I have been also preparing my own trousseau from these items. I have made you the necessary undergarments, but you are right, you will have bare feet in your slippers.'

'That is a mere bagatelle. As long as I am looking like the future wife of a lord, I shall be content.'

* * *

Night had fallen when they left the house to cross the small square. As always the sound of laughing voices travelled through the darkness as families gathered in their courtyards to chat and drink before eating.

'Mama, I had forgotten how inconvenient it is to have skirts to trip over,' Sofia said as she held hers up in front of her.

'You look every inch a lady, my dear daughter, and Perry will be suitably impressed at your transformation I can assure you.'

'His house is ablaze with candlelight – that in itself is strange. Do you think he has invited anyone else to dine with him?'

'I have no more idea than you. We shall both find out in a moment.'

The front door was wide open. There was no need to knock. From the number of voices drifting out from the veranda at the rear of the building they realised they were not the only guests.

She dropped her skirt, shook it vigorously to ensure it had no creases, and walked in ahead of her mother. She had half expected the dog to be the first to greet her but this was not the case.

'My darling, you look *ravissante*. If I thought you would obey me, I would insist that you never wear men's attire again.' Perry took her hand and kissed her knuckles. Then he tucked it through his and turned to nod politely to her mother.

'Welcome, ma'am. As no doubt you can hear there is to be a celebration of more than just family.'

He led her into the main room where there were half a dozen people milling about, all dressed in their best. She and Mama were the only ladies present who did not have their hair dressed with combs and black lace. The gentlemen were in black, but there the resemblance to English evening dress ceased. Their evening jackets were short-waisted and their trousers tight. They wore high-collared white shirts beneath their jackets, and no neckcloths.

Her beloved had from somewhere purchased a dark blue topcoat and a new, startlingly white shirt with lace cuffs that emerged from sleeves and almost covered his hands. His neckcloth was tied elaborately, but he was still wearing his everyday breeches and riding boots – although these had been spruced up.

Don Pablo bowed to Mama and guided her to the far side of the room where they could converse privately.

Perry squeezed her hand. 'You have nothing to worry about, sweetheart; important people in this small town have decided to ignore our indiscretion, to pretend it didn't happen, and this is the announcement of our betrothal. The fact that I am an aristocrat was enough for them to forgive us.'

'Are you quite sure? I haven't dared to look directly at any of the guests.'

'You may do so with impunity, darling girl. All you will receive in return are benevolent smiles.'

Juan appeared with a tray of champagne and she took a glass. Perry stiffened beside her. She glanced up and smiled sweetly. 'Unlike most young ladies of your acquaintance, my love, I have a head for alcohol. I rarely get the opportunity to drink champagne and do not intend to miss out.'

He winked at her, which made her giggle. 'There

is nothing about you that is similar to any girl I've ever come in contact with. You are unique and you are mine.' He almost growled this last phrase and heat pooled in a most unexpected place.

'Behave yourself, my lord, or I shall not be answerable for the consequences.' She had deliberately parroted his words and his expression showed his appreciation of her wit.

He took her up onto the veranda and then turned to face the dozen people assembled in front of him. 'I should like to thank you all for coming tonight to celebrate my extraordinary good fortune. Not only have I regained my identity and my sight today, I have also become betrothed to Miss Sofia Appleby.' He looked down at her and his eyes blazed. 'I would forego both of the former and happily settle for the latter if I was forced to make a choice.'

He raised his glass. 'I give you the future Lady Peregrine Sheldon.'

Everyone echoed his words and drank the toast. Then Don Pablo toasted both of them and they drank again.

Delicious smells were wafting in from the kitchen and her mouth watered. 'Perry, I have not eaten since breakfast. I hope dinner will not be long.'

'We have tapas for the first remove, then a selection of local dishes, and we shall finish with fruit and nuts.'

'Please talk of this no more, but lead me to the table. My stomach will rumble so loudly everyone present will hear it if I do not eat immediately.'

7

Following the French company without being detected was easy as they left a trail of horse dung and dust. They rode their cavalry horses into the ground and so they also left the smell of suppurating saddle-sores behind them.

'Smith, when do you think they will look for somewhere to hide for the day?' They were riding boot to boot and Beau was able to pitch his voice so quietly it was barely audible.

'I reckon just before dawn. They'll not want to be on the track when the sun comes up. I ain't surprised they're travelling at night. I'm going ahead; I'll be back before light. We needs to be clear where they are.'

They continued for another hour and then he noticed that the route ahead was becoming clearer – it would be dawn soon. Beau guided his horses off the route and into a small stony area behind some scrubby trees. The air was full of the scent of herbs and he inhaled appreciatively.

He pulled the reins over the stallion's head and dropped them. This was sufficient to keep the animal close as he had been trained not to wander off when his reins were trailing. All that was left to do was tether the other animal. He waited behind a tree for his companion to return.

How long would it take Jenkins to bring a company of English cavalry? It couldn't be infantry; they couldn't be here soon enough even if they marched in double time. He tensed. There was more than one horseman approaching so it couldn't be Smith. He ducked down behind the trees and backed to his horse. 'Quiet, old fellow, don't make a sound.' He snatched the reins and rested his gloved hand on the animal's nose.

A group of about a dozen mounted men appeared around the corner. It was just light enough to see that Smith wasn't with them, but he was certain they were not French. He was going to let them pass but on closer inspection he was convinced by their fierce appearance and healthy horses that they must be partisans. Of course, not all of the guerrillas fighting the French were prepared to work with the English.

He stepped into full view and greeted them in Spanish. 'Good morning to you. I am Silchester. I have news that might be of interest to you.' He had their full attention. 'I'm also looking for my brother, Lord Peregrine Sheldon. He has been missing somewhere in these hills since July.'

Immediately a ripple of something he didn't recognise travelled through the group. They all dismounted and one man, presumably the leader, walked up to him smiling broadly. He replied in the same tongue. 'You are the Duke of Silchester? We have your brother, Perry, living with us. It's God's will that we have met you in this extraordinary fashion. I am Carlos, son of Don Pablo, and leader of this band.'

Beau gripped the man's outstretched hand fiercely and then embraced him. His throat was thick. He blinked furiously to clear his eyes and sent up a prayer to the Almighty for granting him his dearest wish.

'I knew Perry wasn't dead. Is he badly injured?'

Carlos laughed, the sound echoing off the cliffs

that surrounded them. 'He is healthy, sir, but blind. He doesn't know who he is and will be shocked to discover he's an aristocrat.'

'Then how did you know it is he that I was looking for?' As soon as he asked he knew the question to be ridiculous. There was hardly likely to be more than one Englishman wandering about the place.

'The one thing he did know was that his name was Perry – so mystery solved. What was it you wish to tell us?'

He quickly explained about the French. 'Your man hasn't returned and we didn't any see French on our patrol. Only God Almighty knows where they might be hiding.'

'If you would kindly direct me to your village, I should like to go there immediately and be reunited with my sibling.'

'I shall do better than that – I shall take you myself. My men will go in search of the missing company.' He gave his orders briskly and all but one of them remounted and rode off. The remaining partisan was to wait and bring the cavalry to join the others, wherever they might be.

Beau was not a fighting man, although he would do so if the lives of any of his loved ones or himself was at stake. He rather thought he had disappointed Carlos by not insisting on going in search of the French and joining in the attack that would follow.

'Tell me exactly how my brother came to be with you.' He listened and at the end of the story he knew that he and his family would be forever indebted to this man and his family. He was intrigued by the mention of the English girl and her mother, who were apparently living happily in their midst.

'Why have they not returned to England?'

'They have nothing to go back to. They prefer to make their life with us and they are now part of our town. The Señora Appleby is to marry my father, Don Pablo.' He hesitated and when he spoke again there was sadness in his voice. 'I had hoped to marry Sofia, but she has set her sights on your brother and has no time for me.'

This was not good news. For Perry to have become entangled with someone who might be totally unsuitable could be a problem – but he was sure the matter could be smoothed over if sufficient money was involved.

* * *

Sofia scarcely knew what she had eaten that night, but all of it was delicious. She had drifted – always with Perry at her side – from one group to the next, and everyone had congratulated her and wished her well.

He insisted on walking her home although she was quite capable of completing the journey without his assistance. She rather feared this was his nature, that by marrying him she would spend the rest of her life being taken care of, protected from the slightest injury, and not allowed to make decisions for herself.

'Perry, this is happening too fast. It's entirely my fault, but could I ask you if we could postpone our nuptials for a while until we have had time to adjust to the new circumstances?'

'Absolutely not. You could be carrying my child – we shall be married at the earliest possible opportunity and I'll brook no disagreement on this matter.'

They had now reached her front door. 'Then I must just pray our priest does not arrive for several weeks, as by then it will be clear if I am in the family way. If I am not then there is no necessity for us to marry at all. Goodnight, my lord.'

She skipped inside before he could react to her inflammatory statement and quickly slid the bolt across so he could not barge his way in. She stood quivering behind the door, waiting for his assault. To her chagrin she could definitely hear him whistling as he walked away.

He was infuriating but she wouldn't be coerced into becoming his wife unless she chose to marry him. She unbolted the door, as her mother would have to come in at some point, and turned to dash up the stairs forgetting she was wearing a gown. Her foot went through the hem and she stumbled to her knees. She turned the air blue with her language.

'Sofia Appleby, do not use such words in this house. In fact, my girl, do not use them at all. I can assure you that your future husband will not tolerate such behaviour.'

Her mother had come in and overheard her tirade. Sofia carefully extracted her slipper from the rent in her pretty gown and pushed herself upright. 'I apologise, Mama. As you see I have ruined this dress.'

'It's not spoilt. I can repair it easily enough. It will be dawn in an hour or two so we had better retire and try and get some sleep.'

She couldn't sleep. She tossed and turned and eventually abandoned the attempt. She quickly dressed in her usual masculine garments and quietly let herself out into the square. Perry's house was in darkness. He was having no difficulty sleeping.

There was sufficient light for her to find her way to the corral and call for her gelding. She didn't bother to tack him up. She often rode him bareback and without even a halter to guide him. They were cantering across the vineyard when a grey shape arrived at her side.

'Good morning, Zorro, I should be glad of your company.'

She had been warned by Carlos several times not to go out alone at night – not every Spaniard could be trusted and the French certainly couldn't. No one could object to her riding at dawn now she had this enormous dog at her side.

She guided the horse with her knees and a hand on his neck. They hopped over the stone wall at the end of the vineyard and into the olive groves. Here she had to crouch over his neck in order to avoid being swept from his back. The terraces that surrounded the village were fertile and grew all the food they needed. These had been painstakingly built centuries ago, but the retaining walls were still sound.

She spent an enjoyable hour or so wandering around the terraces and was now a considerable distance from the town. 'We shall go through here and then onto that track up there. It will be light enough to travel safely through the hills soon.'

Her mouth curved as she finished speaking. As if either animal would understand a word she said – but talking to them was how you built up a bond, even if they didn't know exactly what you were saying.

The light was beginning to creep up the hills and soon they would be bathed in early morning sunlight. Perhaps she would be wiser to turn around and go home before the town was awake and her mother realised she had gone out. A faint flicker of unease ran through her as she thought there was someone else who might disapprove more strongly of her behaviour and possibly take stern action to prevent her doing so again.

Just ahead the track split. One half led up to the town and the other down towards the villages a few hours away in which the French had taken up residence. They had fortified them and the partisans no longer attempted to raid in that direction, as it was too dangerous.

The English army would have to remove these clusters of French soldiers if they ever hoped to push on and into France itself. She was lost in her thoughts, not taking notice of her surroundings when suddenly Zorro snarled.

Too late she understood the danger. She wasn't

alone as she had thought and it was too late to turn the horse and escape.

***

Perry was still smiling when he returned to his own home. Life with his darling girl was certainly not going to be dull and he would not have it any other way. He hoped for her sake she wasn't increasing as having a baby arrive several weeks before it's due date caused unpleasant speculation.

He'd told his staff to douse all the candles and lamps as he was comfortable walking around in the dark. He rubbed his eyes and yawned. He might as well turn in. It was going to be a busy day tomorrow as he had heard from the don that the priest would be arriving that afternoon. There were already three other weddings planned and his had been added to the list. The wedding breakfast would be held here, then he would set out in search of his missing friend and comrade: O'Reilly.

It was taking longer for his eyes to clear and give him back his perfect vision than he had hoped. He could see perfectly well when looking forwards but his peripheral vision was definitely impaired. He had to turn his head in order to see anything on either side of him.

If this didn't go then he would be no use as a soldier and would be obliged to resign his commission and return home – but to what? He had a substantial estate a few miles from Silchester Court but that wouldn't keep him occupied. Even being married to Sofia wouldn't be enough to prevent him from becoming bored. Perhaps when Aubrey returned, which he must do eventually, he would take his new bride on a world trip to visit exotic places like India and the Spice Islands.

They were not a family who stood on ceremony but even so his future bride was going to find it extremely difficult becoming the wife of an aristocrat. Making morning calls and attending supper parties would seem tame after the life she had been living these past two years.

He slept well. A soldier learned to sleep when he could and he still had that facility. He was roused by a voice calling him from the bottom of the stairs. Why hadn't his dog barked?

He rolled out of bed and hastily pulled on his breeches as he didn't think his future mother-in-law would appreciate the sight of him buck naked. He was still pulling his shirt on over his head when he reached the head of the stairs.

'Perry, Sofia didn't sleep in her bed last night. Is she with you?'

A lump lodged in his stomach. 'No, she's not.' He was busy tucking in his shirt as he spoke. 'Give me a moment, ma'am, whilst I finish dressing and then I will be downstairs and you will have my full attention.'

Another thing a soldier could do was dress and be ready to fight in minutes – often lives depended on his speed. Only officers bothered to remove their outer garments; troops slept in what they had on. Small wonder the smell of unwashed bodies followed the army around.

'I'm ready. Have you checked her horse is there? I know that Sofia likes to ride at dawn. In fact, I'm certain she has gone out on her horse and taken my dog with her.'

He ran to the paddocks and checked the tack room, then realised he didn't know which saddle and bridle belonged to her as he had never seen it. However, he didn't need to know as there were none missing from the pegs.

Mrs Appleby arrived, puffing and red-faced. 'Does

Sofia ever ride without tack? Do you know which of these horses belongs to her?'

'I don't know about riding bareback – I've certainly never seen her do so – but then I'm rarely down here as I am not overfond of horses. I couldn't tell you which one is hers as they all look the same to me. You need to ask one of the men.'

Perry raced back to the town and hammered on the door of Don Pablo. It was opened immediately by a serving maid. He ignored her and stepped in shouting for attention. Nobody got up early in Spain so he directed his yell up the stairs.

A few moments later the don appeared in his nightshirt with his hair unkempt. 'This had better be urgent, my lord. I do not take kindly to being disturbed so early in the morning.'

Once he had explained the urgency, everything changed. 'I'll be with you in a moment, Perry, my son. I have a very bad feeling about this. She should have been back at first light as she never stays away so long that she worries her mother.'

'It's a damned nuisance the young men are already out as we could do with their help to search for her. Have there been reports of French activity nearby?'

'This is what my men have gone to investigate.

The English army is moving forward and attempting to drive the enemy from our land as they did for the Portuguese. We are doing everything we can to assist. We have suffered enough over the past few years at the hands of those bastards and want our country back again.'

'I'll get our horses saddled. I have my pistol but I wish I had a sword.'

'Wait there. I can supply you with one. I shall be but a few minutes dressing. There is little point in you going ahead.'

Perry prowled around the entrance hall, impatient to be off. Why was it that nothing happened for weeks and then everything changed? The priest would be here by lunchtime and they were supposed to be married soon after. His future mother-in-law was already in the process of arranging a second celebration. He had intended that he and Sofia would leave the following morning, hopefully with at least two or three of the fierce partisans if they had returned in time.

True to his word, Don Pablo clattered down the stairs a few minutes later. 'This way, my son – the armoury is at the rear of the house.'

He was handed a magnificent Toledo steel blade, the hilt beautifully engraved and the scabbard covered in emerald green leather. He held it reverently before buckling it around his waist.

'I thank you, sir. I shall take good care of it and return it in good order.'

'It is yours to keep, my wedding gift to you.'

Although his companion was twenty years his senior he appeared much younger and was able to move as fast as Perry was. Perry whistled for his horse and the animal cantered over.

'Now, that is a useful trick. I shall suggest that in future we train our animals to react in the same way.'

Marron was ready first but objected strenuously when he attempted to mount with his sword swinging at his waist. By the time he had calmed the beast and managed to scramble into the saddle, the don was also mounted.

'It will be full light shortly. If anything untoward has taken place we need to have discovered it before then. Follow me. I know the route that she often takes on her dawn rides.'

They dodged and wove through the olives and the vines for what seemed like miles before eventually emerging onto a well-worn track.

'I am most concerned that we haven't seen any sign of her. I expected to find her injured somewhere with her horse beside her. This is where my land ends.' He pointed with his whip. 'If you continue in that direction it will eventually take you to the next town. In the other, if you travel far enough, you will come across the first of the villages the French have occupied and fortified.'

Perry stood in his stirrups and could see that the track divided a few hundred yards ahead in the direction that led to the French. 'Where does the other route go?'

'Eventually it will lead back to our town, but it climbs before it meanders in the right direction. I think we should investigate that before we try either of the other paths.'

8

Beau followed his guide for several miles and then he was looking down into a small valley between the foothills and saw the town. This was a relief as his shoulder was aching from being obliged to lead the spare horse. This place was bigger than he'd expected, more prosperous, and obviously hadn't been targeted by the French for some reason. Possibly this was because it wasn't on the direct route that the soldiers took and wasn't worth the effort.

As far as he knew the French army stole what they needed and from what he could see there was plenty of food available down there. He called out to the young man in front, 'I'm curious as to why the French have allowed you to prosper when they are constantly looking for supplies.'

Carlos reined in and swung round in his saddle. 'We are sufficiently far off the beaten track for them not to be aware of us. They have taken over or destroyed most of the villages an hour or so away, but so far we've been lucky.' He smiled, his teeth white in his tanned face. 'It also helps that we have made sure we stay put when they are marching across the hills.'

'I assume there are several better tracks that they can use.'

'There are, sir, and the bulk of the Frenchies are now on the other side of the mountains – thank the good Lord for that. The next army that will pass will be yours and they don't strip the land but pay their way.'

There was smoke coming from several chimneys and he could hear goats bleating, dogs barking and children crying. The houses were stone-built, looked sturdy. There was a small square with a well surrounded by the larger houses and then a second marketplace where the dwellings were less substantial.

Both the marketplace and the smaller square were dotted with people going about their business. He hoped Perry would be as delighted to see him... He winced inwardly. His younger sibling might never be able to actually see him. This was a tragedy for a young man who was so active, who had made his life in the military.

This must be why he had developed a fondness for the English girl. Perhaps, in the circumstances, he would not interfere in this matter but let the two of them make a match of it, if that is what they wanted. If she was prepared to take him penniless and blind then she must truly love him.

He looked around with interest as they approached what had been Perry's home for the past few months. Sylvester pricked his ears and increased his pace. The gelding behind was not so eager and Beau's shoulder was almost dislocated.

This horse was unlikely to wander off now they were so close to civilisation, so he released the reins and trusted to the animal's good sense. He flexed his shoulder and hoped he'd not done it any permanent damage.

The townspeople paused and stared at him as he rode past. He was used to being the centre of attention and ignored it. No doubt his stallion was impressing them; they were unlikely to have such superb horse-flesh in this neck of the woods. The fact that there was a second riderless, equally magnificent, beast trotting along behind him must also be arousing their curiosity.

Carlos led him to the smaller square, which he had seen from above. The man pointed to a modest house. 'That is where your brother resides. I'll leave you to introduce yourself. Allow me to take your horses and see to their needs.'

Beau dismounted and handed over the reins. His companion had already collected Billy, the bay that he had brought over for his brother, and had no difficulty leading the two away even though they towered over his smaller mount.

Only as they disappeared did he realise he had left his belongings on Billy. He could hardly yell after the man – that would be unconscionable. He would send someone to fetch them shortly – he could manage perfectly well without his things for the moment.

He smiled wryly as he strode across to knock on the door of the house that his brother had been residing in for the past few weeks. It was quite possible there wouldn't be a *someone* to send. He waited impatiently but no one answered the door.

Then a woman called him and he turned around to see an attractive woman of middle years, dressed in the Spanish way, hurrying towards him. 'Are you looking for Perry?' She stopped and her cheeks coloured. She dipped in a formal curtsy, much to his embarrassment. 'I beg your pardon, your grace, I can see now the resemblance to Lord Peregrine.'

He bowed, hoping to demonstrate he wasn't so high in the instep as to expect the people here to bow and scrape to him. 'And you must be Mrs Appleby. Carlos explained to me that you and your daughter saved my brother's life. I take it he is elsewhere.'

'Please, your grace, will you come to my humble abode and I shall tell you what I know. I am sure you would like to freshen up and eat and drink before you go in search of him.'

Beau was mystified as to how his brother would need to be searched for when he was blind. All this could be explained to him when they were out of the sun, which was already unpleasantly hot, even at this time in the morning.

'Forgive me, ma'am, but I must fetch my saddle bags. Stupidly I let them disappear with my horse...'

She spoke rapidly to a boy fetching water at the well. He understood enough to know that she was sending him to fetch his things.

'Thank you, I should now be delighted to accompany you.'

The inside of her house was cool, the thick stone walls keeping out the heat. It was surprisingly spacious, and was twice as long as it was wide. 'If you would care to follow me, your grace, there is a washroom at the rear of my house. You will find everything you need in there. If you require any other facilities, they are next door.'

Apart from having to duck his head when entering the washroom he found it to be perfectly adequate. What he would really like was to have a strip wash under a pump, but he could hardly do that here as the water was carried in buckets from the well. Also, he needed his clothes before he could remove his soiled garments.

There was a polite knock on the door scarcely five minutes after he'd arrived and the youth bowed and handed him the saddle bags. Even something as simple as washing filled him with pleasure. He rather thought he had been tense ever since he'd had the news that Perry was missing. Knowing his brother was safe, and relatively well, removed the weight from his shoulders. There was no longer any need for urgency and he was quite happy to take his time over his ablutions.

When he emerged a considerable time later Mrs Appleby appeared above him on a balcony that ran the width of the house. 'If you would care to join me here, sir, I have refreshments ready.'

As there was no sign of the daughter – Sofia he thought she was called – he must suppose that she was out somewhere with his brother. He would make polite enquiries about this family whilst he ate. Mrs Appleby was perfectly acceptable; she had good manners and excellent diction. Her garb might be a tad outlandish, but it was hardly surprising she had chosen to blend in.

He found his way to the veranda and could see why she had suggested they sit there. The entire area was shaded and looked out over the valley and towards what he supposed would be France somewhere on the other side of the mountains.

'This looks and smells quite delicious. This will be the first meal I have eaten using cutlery and crockery for several days.'

'I imagine eating around a campfire is not something you are accustomed to, your grace.'

'How true, ma'am, but despite what you might think of me, I have actually enjoyed the experience.' He took a bite of the delicious pie and then became more interested in his food than in the conversation. The impromptu meal was washed down with a tart, dry cider.

'That was excellent. I am replete. Might I now ask exactly where my brother is? I assume he is with your daughter as he could not be wandering about the place on his own.'

Her smile was triumphant. 'He recovered his memory and his sight yesterday. Did you not think it strange that I knew your name and that you were a duke?'

His jaw dropped at his stupidity. He had been so overjoyed at the thought of seeing his beloved brother again the significance of her using his title had gone over his head. Then the true implication of her first sentence registered. 'He isn't blind? He knows who he is? I can't believe what I'm hearing. Carlos obviously was unaware of this fact or he would have told me himself.'

'The men had already left when this happened. Now, Perry... I beg your pardon, Lord Peregrine...'

'Please continue to address my brother as you have always done. Do not stand on ceremony for me.'

'Perry has gone in search of Sofia. You must understand that things are done differently here, especially since the war began so many years ago. She rides out with the partisans, wears men's clothing, and has the same freedom as the young men. She often rides at dawn when it is cooler and must have done so today, but she has failed to return at her usual time.'

His joy changed to concern. 'There is a French company travelling through the pass not far from here. They are transporting coinage, no doubt to pay the troops. I hope to God she did not come in contact with them.'

* * *

An unkempt man emerged from the bushes and snatched her from her horse's back. Sofia opened her mouth to scream but he put his hand across it and dragged her back until they were both hidden from the track.

'Hush, missy, no need for all the fuss. I'll not hurt you.'

He spoke English and immediately she stopped struggling. 'I am Sofia Appleby. Who might you be?'

His gap-toothed grin was infectious and she returned his smile. 'I'm Jeremiah Smith, miss, at your service. What the bleedin' hell are you doing out here on your own?'

They were now in a hollow away from the track and she could see his horse tethered close by. She was about to insist she went in search of her own mount when there was the sound of hooves and Pedro pushed his way through the dense thicket and happily trotted over to join the much larger animal.

Again Smith swore and she couldn't restrain her intake of breath. He chuckled and touched his forehead. 'Beggin' your pardon, miss, barrack-room language. Was a soldier until I did my time and found myself a comfortable billet back in England.'

'And I apologise for being ridiculous. I take it there are French soldiers ahead and that is why you brought me here?'

'The buggers are a couple of hundred yards from here. If you'd gone much further you would have been seen by their sentry. Dressed like you are, I reckon they'd not have treated you like a lady.'

His blunt words sent a shiver down her spine. He'd no need to elaborate as she knew exactly what happened to Spanish women unfortunate enough to be captured by the French. Smith explained what he was doing there and who he was travelling with.

'Perry's brother is here? The Duke of Silchester himself? He will be overjoyed to find him fully recovered.' She was about to say that his grace might well not be so pleased about discovering she was to marry into the family today, then realised this would be a highly unsuitable conversation to have with a man who was obviously a servant of some sort from the way he spoke.

'I fear that Perry might well come in search of me. He cannot be allowed to blunder into the French. They would shoot him on sight.'

'Don't you fret, missy. I'll not let that happen. You stop here along with the horses; you'll be safe enough. What direction will Lord Peregrine be coming from?'

She pointed and he nodded. 'I'm an ex-rifleman, a skirmisher. I can move about without being seen if I have to. I'll make my way back and stop him before he's in any danger.'

'The English cavalry could be here at any time. I'm praying that he might see them and discover for himself what is going on.'

He didn't answer and disappeared through the low-growing scrub, leaving her alone. If her foolish-ness led the man she loved into danger, she would never forgive herself. The horses were happily grazing and didn't need her attention. She had not been sit-ting in the hollow for very long when she began to feel uncomfortable.

Attending to the call of nature when one was dressed in a gown was relatively simple even when outdoors; however, doing so when in breeches was another thing altogether. It required that she expose a part of her anatomy that was best kept out of sight. She could not possibly empty her bladder when at any moment Smith could return or, even worse, bring with him the man she hoped to marry very soon.

Soon the matter became so urgent she had no choice. She could hardly do what needed to be done where she was sitting as the wet patch would be immediately obvious. That would be too humiliating – it would also be unpleasant to sit in.

She had been told to remain where she was and to remain quiet. The horses were presumably in a safe place so it should be permissible for her to go to join them. She slithered down on her bottom, not wishing to raise her head any higher than necessary.

'Keep still, boys. I'll not disturb you much.' She patted both the animals in turn and was then relieved and delighted to find there was a convenient space behind a large rock that she could utilise. Once she was comfortable she quickly tucked her shirt tails between her legs and pulled up her breeches.

Not a moment too soon as Smith, accompanied by

two men from the village, crawled into view. She prayed they would think she had gone down to check on the welfare of the horses and that they wouldn't notice her pink cheeks. Keeping in a crouched position, she went to join them.

'You need to leave, miss. You can take one of these men's horses. They'll use yours when they want to return,' Smith told her.

'I shall be glad to go. I don't want to be in the middle of a pitched battle. I shall wait for Perry and make sure he comes with me. I've no wish for him to be involved either; he's not fully recovered yet.'

One of the men remained with Smith and the other accompanied her back to the path where he tossed her into the saddle. The stirrup leathers had already been shortened, so she rammed her boots into the irons and was ready to leave.

'Joseph, where are the rest of the men?'

He gestured with his head and she saw what she had missed before, that the remaining partisans were stealthily moving through the scrub so they could fire down on the French when the English cavalry arrived and charged them from the front.

Once they were safely away she reined in, determined to remain where she was and wait for her beloved to appear. From her vantage point she could see in all directions without being seen herself. The sun was fully up and it was going to be another baking hot day – unusual for the beginning of autumn.

'Look, I can see Don Pablo and that must be Perry riding with him. Good Lord, he looks ready for battle. He's wearing a sword around his waist.'

She stood in her stirrups and waved until she attracted their attention. It would be simpler for them to come to her rather than the other way around, as the track in front of her was the most direct one back to the town. He arrived at her side and did not look particularly pleased to see her. She spoke first hoping her good news would soften his mood.

'Perry, your brother, the duke, has arrived to take you home. There is a French company a mile away and they are carrying chests of gold. Jenkins has gone to fetch the English cavalry and Smith is keeping watch.'

'And you have been doing exactly what these past few hours?'

'Smith saved me from blundering into the French camp and I have been hiding with him until it was safe to leave.'

Her words made him look even grimmer. He had come armed to the teeth in her defence when he should have been resting at home. Her stupidity had ruined what should have been a wonderful day.

'I am so sorry. I shall fully understand if you no longer wish to marry me this afternoon.'

He looked at her as if she was speaking in tongues and then stretched out and lifted her bodily from the saddle and placed her in front of him. 'The sooner I marry you the better, my girl. You are running wild at the moment and I intend to put a stop to that.'

She opened her mouth to protest but he closed it with a kiss that made her forget everything apart from how much she loved him. When he raised his head, his eyes told her everything she needed to know. Whatever she did, however badly she behaved, he would always love her even when he was enraged by her outlandish ways.

'We shall return. I've no wish to join in the fight today or, alas, any other day.' He turned his gelding's head and kicked him into a canter. Sitting sideways on the pommel was extremely uncomfortable and only his arms around her waist kept her in place. There was no point in protesting as she thought he was doing it deliberately. She hoped this would be her only punishment.

They were only halfway back when she heard the sound of two horses approaching at speed from behind. She peered around Perry's shoulder. 'It's Smith and another man who must be Jenkins. The cavalry has arrived and the French are about to be routed.' She had been obliged to shout but she was pretty sure he heard her although he didn't respond.

When he reined in at the paddock he tipped her unceremoniously to the ground and she barely kept her feet. 'I shall see you at the church in one hour from now. Do not be late – tardiness is something I cannot abide.'

She moved swiftly out of his reach before turning. 'And I cannot abide overbearing, arrogant aristocrats, but I suppose we must both endure as we have no choice in the matter.'

The sound of his laughter followed her and she was tempted to turn a cartwheel but thought that might be a step too far.

'There you are. I knew you would arrive in time to prepare for your wedding.' Mama didn't mention the fact that she had been missing for hours, or that they now not only had a lord, but a duke in their midst.

Sofia stood in a basin whilst her mother tipped warm water over her and then rubbed her from top to toe in their precious orange blossom soap. 'What about you? You must have time to get ready as well.'

'I have only to take off this old gown and put on

my wedding finery and I am done. I hope you like the gown I sewed for this special day.'

Draped over the end of her bed was the most beautiful gown she had ever seen. It was in palest green, high-waisted, with a full train of organza and edged with beading. Strictly speaking it was an evening gown, but it was perfect for a wedding too.

'I love it. I shall look like a real bride wearing that.' She examined it more closely and saw there was a loop of material hidden under the train so she could put this over her wrist and thus keep the train from under her feet.

'Of course you are a real bride. Good heavens, child, you are marrying the brother of the Duke of Silchester. I should think that Perry must be one of the most eligible bachelors in England and yet here we are about to welcome him to our humble family.'

'You have met the duke? What is he like?'

'He is a dark version of your future husband. He is slightly taller and broader but quite definitely his brother. I have never conversed with someone so toplofty before but found him quite charming and pleasant.'

'I am rather dreading walking down the aisle on my own. I...'

'That is not going to happen, my love. Don Pablo

will escort you. After all we are to be married to-morrow ourselves so he's almost your papa.'

'To think that yesterday there were only the two of us in the family and tomorrow I shall have a host of brothers and sisters, a husband, and a new father.'

9

Perry unbuckled his sword and rammed it in the scabbard. He would never wear it again. His days of soldiering were done. There were half a dozen women cleaning his house from top to bottom and preparing it for the wedding breakfast to be held in a couple of hours. Where the hell was Beau?

The wedding gift he'd received from the don must be returned. It would just be a constant reminder of what he had lost. If the injury had occurred during a battle he would not feel so angry about the damage to his eyes. To be forced to give up what he loved most because of a stupid accident was hard to accept.

The door to the don's grand house was opened

and he could hear his brother's voice inside. He walked in and saw Beau deep in conversation with his future father-in-law. As he hadn't announced his arrival, they were unaware he was observing them.

His eyes filled. He was a veritable watering pot lately. A servant appeared at his side and he handed him the sword. 'Put this in the armoury.' He'd spoken quietly so he wouldn't be heard on the veranda where the other two were talking.

He strode forward to greet his brother. 'Beau, how in God's name did you find me? You should never have come. Risking your life when you are head of the family was...' He got no further as he was embraced fiercely. His brother's eyes were as moist as his.

'Perry, I knew you were not dead. I haven't slept comfortably since I heard you were missing back in the summer. Did you know that Giselle is now married to Rushton? Beth has just married her lieutenant – I brought her out with me and left her with the army.'

'Both pieces of information are new to me. In an hour from now you will be the only one of us not married.'

'I have told you before that I have no intention of stepping into parson's mousetrap. I have a surfeit of heirs so there's no danger that the family name will not continue after my demise.'

Perry gripped his shoulders. 'Good God, I'm not suggesting you marry because you have to but because you will be happier sharing your life with a woman you love.'

'I am four and thirty soon, brother, and if I have not fallen in love so far I think it highly unlikely I shall do so in the future. Good God, I've met hundreds of hopeful young ladies. If I was meant to become enamoured then it would have happened already.'

'In which case your siblings will set about finding you the perfect bride. I shall need something to occupy my time once I am home.'

He quickly explained why he would have to resign his commission and Beau was suitably sympathetic. 'I think it's a shame that your Sofia is not to become a soldier's bride, as I think she will be far better suited to that position than our cousin Beth.'

'Have you met her yet?'

'I have not had the pleasure. If she is as pleasant as her mother then I shall be more than satisfied to have her in the family.'

'God's teeth! I don't give a damn whether you are

satisfied. I remember your reaction when Bennett wanted to marry someone you believed was unsuitable – I thought you had changed, but obviously I am wrong.' Perry immediately regretted his angry outburst. What the hell was wrong with him? In less than an hour he was to marry the girl who would make his life complete, so why wasn't he in high alt?

'I beg your pardon, Beau, I'm out of sorts today. Excuse me, I must change my clothes. I cannot appear at the church in my dirt.'

'I shall come with you. There are still many things we must talk about and I doubt you will have the time or inclination to do so after the ceremony.'

'I can't return to England immediately, Beau. I must find my orderly, O'Reilly, who I think has been captured. Will you and your men accompany me on this search?'

His brother smiled. 'Hardly a romantic wedding trip, but no doubt it will suit the pair of you very well. I should be delighted to accompany you as long as you give me your word that as soon as you have discovered what happened to O'Reilly you will return with me to England?'

'I have nowhere else to go. Sofia and I will have to stay at Silchester until the tenants leave my estate. I can hardly throw them out when they have been exemplary.'

They continued the conversation whilst Perry was completing his ablutions in the washroom.

'I have a suggestion to make. Would you and Sofia consider making your home permanently with me? Aubrey and Mary intend to do so, and I have converted the east wing for their use. I could do the same for the west for you and your new bride.'

Perry didn't hesitate. 'I should like nothing better. Silchester is a vast establishment and will do better having three families living there. If you are not to set up your own nursery then you no doubt will be overrun with nieces and nephews eventually.'

Juan had put out the blindingly white, overdecorated and ridiculous shirt that his temporary valet insisted was essential for a wedding. There were black trousers to accompany this nonsense that were so tight he feared the slightest movement would rip the seams.

He refused point-blank to wear the gold embroidered jacket that should complete the outfit. 'I'll wear my new topcoat so you can put that hideous object away.'

His hair had grown to below collar length, so he tied it at the nape of his neck with a strip of black ribbon. Not so many years ago the common soldier had been forced to have a tarred pigtail, and even gentlemen had worn their hair in this way.

'Don't scowl at me, Beau. I shall have it cut when I get home.'

His brother was gazing out of the window. 'Your guests are already on their way to the church. If we do not leave now you will be late.'

'That I must not be, as I told Sofia I could not tolerate tardiness.'

'What was her response to your remark?'

When he told him they both laughed. If he couldn't be a soldier then he would endeavour to be a good husband and hopefully one day a good parent too. He was about to set out when he noticed the sword he had returned was leaning against the wall just inside the door. It would be churlish to refuse it a second time.

* * *

'Your future husband and his handsome brother have just left for the church. We must depart ourselves in the next few minutes if we are not to be late. In honour of the duke your wedding is the first of four to be held today.'

'I do hope we don't have to sit through an interminable Mass, Mama. I much prefer the shorter service that we get in our own church. Father Benedict will be there until midnight if everyone has the nuptial Mass. As long as we are legally married I have no wish to prolong the ceremony.' She shook out nonexistent creases in her beautiful gown. 'It is a shame they can never ring the church bells for fear that the French would be attracted here.'

'I understand from Don Pablo that the other couples are being married simultaneously to avoid that problem. For your marriage to be recognised in Spain, it must be conducted as it always is. You will have to sit through an even more elaborate ceremony tomorrow morning when it will be my turn.'

Now was not the time to mention that Perry had said they would leave at dawn to begin the search for his missing comrade. To be honest, she had no desire to see her mother marry the Spaniard, as this would mean she might never see her again. Mama should have been able to accompany her back to England to join in her good fortune.

The small square was deserted. No doubt everyone was in the church. Somehow it didn't seem right to be walking just with her mother, surely the don should have accompanied them? The closer she got the less enthusiastic she felt about the whole thing. Was there still time to run away?

Then they emerged into the marketplace and instead of remaining at the altar Perry was striding towards her. His smile squashed her doubts. He loved her, she loved him, whatever life threw at them they could deal with it.

'My darling, I refused to sit in a church full of strangers. I wish we could wait until we could be married at home with my family around us.'

'As this is to be a Catholic ceremony, perhaps we could repeat it in our own religion?'

The tall, dark gentleman waiting by the door must be the duke. He bowed and his expression was warm. 'I am delighted to meet you, and think your suggestion that you have a second marriage at Silchester to be an excellent one.'

She curtsied, not something she could remember doing before. She had never had a Season in London where one was forever bobbing up and down. 'I would have known you for Perry's brother, your grace. Your colouring is dissimilar but in every other way you are the same.'

There was still no sign of the gentleman who she was supposed to be walking down the aisle with and she thought this rather odd. The duke offered his arm and she took it. Perry winked and was about to vanish inside to take up his designated position by the altar when the distant crackle of gunfire echoed from the hills. Not an auspicious start to anyone's married life.

The long, elaborate service was conducted at a leisurely pace and in Spanish. She responded when prompted and when the gold band slipped over her knuckle she was glad it was done and they could get back into the sunshine. It was dark and cold inside the church as it had not been used for years.

Then they were obliged to follow the priest to the altar and kneel for another interminable hour. All she could think about was that Don Pablo had not attended and this was most unlike him. Eventually they were allowed to stand and turned to face the congregation.

Mama was also absent. A sick dread gripped her stomach and she glanced at her husband. He too looked worried. 'Something is wrong. We must go at once and see why my mother and the don did not attend.'

The duke overheard her whispered comment, nodded at his brother and then strode away ahead of them. They were obliged to stop and accept congratulations all the way down the aisle. When they emerged into the sunshine the firing had stopped.

She prayed the English had been successful and that none of the men from the town had been injured.

'Everyone is following us. We cannot abandon our guests. I hope your brother returns speedily to tell us what is happening.'

'Like you, sweetheart, I am concerned at their absence. I'm certain your mother would not have missed your wedding unless it was for something serious.'

There were branches of orange blossom formed into an arch over the doorway. His house was sparkling, the doors to the veranda wide open and in the courtyard a small band of musicians was playing lively music. The wooden steps that led down to the veranda had also been decorated with flowers and blossom. It looked enchanting, she should be happy, but the worry about the missing couple was squashing her joy.

Cider and wine were flowing, a suckling pig had been roasted on a spit in the yard, and a long trestle set up with appetising salads and accompaniments. Once all the guests were happily circulating she and Perry were able to slip away to the far end of the drawing room where they could talk.

'Why hasn't your brother come back? He has been gone this age.'

'We can hardly abandon the wedding breakfast to

go in search of them. I shall send Juan to enquire if I can find him amongst the throng.'

Then the duke appeared and smiled. The initial worry that the older gentleman had succumbed to an apoplexy was removed, but for them to be absent must mean something else had occurred.

'Good, I'm glad that you are here. Don Pablo had distressing news from a messenger who arrived just before your wedding started.

'He has family in a small village higher in the hills and it seems a band of deserters, comprising of both French and English, has invaded the place and taken control. Many of the men were killed and the women and children are now enslaved.'

'They must get word to whoever is leading the English cavalry and have them go at once to their rescue.'

'Exactly so, Perry. Don Pablo has already sent word to them. He intends to meet up with his son and his men in the hills, which is why he didn't attend your wedding. Mrs Appleby left the church because she thought her future husband had suffered an accident or something worse. She will be joining you here as soon as she can.'

Sofia looked anxiously at her new husband but he shook his head. 'No, sweetheart, my soldiering days are over. I shall leave it to men better equipped than I to do the rescuing.'

'Does that mean we are not to go in search of your missing friend before we begin the long journey to the coast?'

'It does not. We shall leave at dawn as planned. I am doing no more than Beau did for me.'

'I feel I must point out, little brother, that O'Reilly is not related to you so perhaps does not require your personal intervention.'

'O'Reilly has been with me since the start. I have spent more time with him in the past two years than with any other person. He would do the same for me. I shall brook no argument on this.'

His brother shrugged and changed the subject. 'Sofia, from this I take it you have no intention of attending the nuptials of your parent?'

'I know it sounds undutiful, but as my mother was prepared to miss my own wedding then I feel no obligation to attend hers.' This sounded shallow and petty but it was too late to retract. The two men exchanged disapproving glances, which made her decide not to explain what she had actually meant.

She had married into this family and must make the best of it, but she had no intention of becoming a subservient wife, however much that infuriated Perry.

What the duke thought of the matter was no concern of hers – she had married Perry, not him, and he must learn to keep his opinions to himself.

The day was spoiled and no amount of merriment could mend it. Her mother arrived full of apologies but it was too late for that. Sofia smiled as if she forgave her, but she didn't. To miss one's only daughter's marriage for such a flimsy reason was inexcusable. She couldn't wait to leave this place. Mama had made her priorities clear – a future husband was more important to her than her own flesh and blood.

* * *

The celebrations went on into the small hours but Sofia complained of having a headache and retired long before the last guests departed. Beau joined Perry on the veranda before they went up.

'I am sorry that this has not been the happy event you had hoped for. You will be having a second ceremony and I shall make sure this one is memorable for the right reasons.'

'I am disappointed in her. I thought her kinder. She will regret departing tomorrow without setting things right with her mother.'

'The French will be gone from Spain soon and

then Don Pablo and Mrs Appleby will be able to travel to England. If you are determined to leave at dawn we had better get some shut-eye first.'

They both knew the marriage would not be consummated tonight, as Sofia had made it quite clear she would be unavailable. They had the rest of their lives to be intimate; he was prepared to wait until she was ready, however long it took.

He had no regrets about marrying her, but he did have worries that the union might not be as harmonious as he would like. He loved her, but wasn't sure that would be enough once they were back in the more restrictive environment of Silchester.

He didn't go into the marital bedroom; he took another empty chamber, stripped off his clothes and fell naked into bed. As he was drifting off to sleep a fact that he had been trying to ignore came to the forefront of his mind.

If he had met Sofia in different circumstances he would never have become involved with her. She was the opposite of everything he had imagined his future wife would be. She was wild, dressed and behaved more like a young man than a young lady of quality, and he doubted she would fit comfortably into his life once they were in England.

He was a gentleman, he had made love to her, he

had had no option but to marry her afterwards. He would have done so even if he had disliked her, so the fact that he loved her to distraction was a definite bonus. No doubt with his guidance and the examples of her sisters-in-law she would adapt to her new life and become the bride he had dreamed of having.

10

Sofia heard Perry walk past the bedroom and her heart broke. He couldn't have made it plainer. He was regretting this marriage as much as she was. If only he had agreed to wait until she saw she had her monthly courses before insisting they tied the knot.

Perhaps if she was not increasing they could have the Catholic service set aside? He must be thinking the same thing, which was why he hadn't joined her. As long as she made sure she kept him at arm's length until they were in England and she could consult a lawyer, it might be possible for her to return to Spain.

Tears trickled down her face. There was nothing for her here; she would never come back. So, if she was not to be Lady Peregrine then she would be forced to throw herself on the mercy of her grand-mother. She shuddered at the thought. She would rather be with Perry, however difficult this might be, than forced to marry someone she didn't love.

At least they had strong feelings for each other even if they were both regretting their hasty marriage. There were so many things she hadn't discussed with Perry – she had no notion where she was to live, how he would occupy his time in future and what his ex-pectations were for her.

This was something they would discuss when they could be alone together. Going in search of this Irishman would be an exciting adventure, something to remember when she was trapped inside a pretty gown pretending to be something she was not.

The following morning she was down and ready to leave before the men arrived. She greeted them as if there was nothing wrong. 'Good morning, I have packed food for the journey, and your breakfast is waiting for you on the veranda. I have already eaten mine.'

Perry strolled across and kissed her on the fore-head. Hardly a passionate embrace, but exactly what she wanted. 'Have you got your belongings? If not, you will need to return to your mother's house and fetch them.'

'I've already done so, and Smith and Jenkins are preparing the horses as we speak. Marron is to be used as the packhorse now that you have such a magnificent animal to ride, Perry. Hopefully, Zorro will be able to keep up with us.'

The duke smiled warmly. 'Then all we have to do is take our own saddle bags with us and we are ready to depart.'

'Juan has already done that, your grace...'

'Enough of the formality, my dear. You are my sister now and I shall call you by your given name and you must do the same for me.'

Perry laughed, a welcome sound, and it made her feel a little more cheerful. 'You have thought of everything, sweetheart. Is there any need to enquire if the necessary equipment has been added to our personal belongings?'

'There is no need. Smith and Jenkins have taken care of that. I heard that the attack on the French yesterday was successful and the English have the gold. It has been sent back to Wellington with an escort, and the remainder of the cavalry have joined Don Pablo and the partisans to take care of the deserters.'

This information was received without comment from either of them. She had expected them to be pleased, but they appeared more interested in their breakfast than in what she had told them.

* * *

She rode away from the town she had spent the past two years in without any regrets. Her new life was with Perry. Hopefully they would be blessed with a large family and this would occupy her time and give her something useful to do.

There was no one around to see them depart, to wave goodbye, and the further they travelled the more she regretted her childish decision not to wake her mother and say goodbye. Too late to repine. She would write a loving letter as soon as she had the opportunity and repeat the invitation for Don Pablo and Mama to make a prolonged stay in England.

Perry had chosen to ride alongside his brother and they were leading the small cavalcade; Smith was leading Marron so Jenkins had taken up position next to her. The hound loped along beside her and she was glad of his company.

'Jenkins, my husband appears to know the direction to go in. Am I to assume he has had information about the whereabouts of this O'Reilly?'

'He's heard from one of the partisans about a

band of roving French cavalry now living in a deserted village. They have half a dozen English prisoners who are being used as orderlies, grooms and such.'

'There are only five of us. How does he think we can rescue his friend against so large a number?'

'Beggin' your pardon, my lady, I don't reckon his lordship expects you to be part of this venture.'

Being addressed for the first time by her new title was disturbing. She had been Sofia to everyone in the town, but now she was someone else entirely. She intended to make the most of the next few weeks of comparative freedom and, whatever Perry and his brother thought, she was going to be part of this rescue.

'Can you fire that rifle from the saddle, Jenkins?' Better to change the subject than argue with one of the duke's servants.

'No, my lady, it's best to be on the ground.'

'I see. Do you know how far away this village is?'

'A day's ride, ma'am, no more than that.'

She squeezed and her horse moved smoothly into a canter so that she caught up with Perry and his brother. 'I should like to ride with my husband, Beau, so could I ask you to drop back?' He guided his stallion to one side and allowed her to pass. No words were exchanged and she thought this odd. What had they been talking about that made them both look so grim?

Her heart was thudding. For the first time since she'd met him she was nervous about speaking to Perry. Then he reached over and took her hand and raised it to his lips the way he always did. His eyes told her all she needed to know.

'I was hoping you would come and join me, sweetheart. I expect you have questions about our future together.'

'Actually, I'm more interested in how you intend to rescue your man when we will be seriously outnumbered.'

'We have the element of surprise, but far more important, I have two of the best marksmen the army has ever produced. Jenkins and Smith will make this work for us if it comes to a fight.'

'I see that you are wearing that sword again. I thought you returned it.'

'I did, but Don Pablo sent it back. I'm glad that he did, because it might well come in useful.' He released her hand and his smile was sad. 'I have to tell you that my vision is still impaired. I can see well enough looking forward, but nothing at all on either side unless I turn my head. Therefore, you will not be obliged to follow the drum after all.'

'You told me that yesterday when you said you would no longer be a soldier. I wish it were otherwise for both of us, as I don't think you will enjoy being a gentleman of leisure any more than I will enjoy being a pampered wife with little to do.'

'There is nothing we can do so we must accept what we cannot change. We are to live at Silchester Court with Beau. My twin, Aubrey, will reside in the east wing when he returns from his gallivanting around the globe and we still take the west. The house is so vast we could go a month and never see each other unless we wished to.'

For a horrible moment she thought he was referring to himself and her. Her shock registered on her face and he laughed out loud, causing his magnificent horse to shy. He dealt with the situation whilst continuing the conversation as if nothing untoward was taking place.

'I am, you pea-goose, referring to not being obliged to see anyone apart from ourselves if we do not wish to. I am fond of my family, but have no intention of living in their pockets.'

'You must tell me about all of them. I am looking forward to being part of a big family and having a plethora of brothers and sisters as well as nieces and nephews to mingle with.'

He told her everything she wanted to know and by the end she could almost believe she had met each one of them, so vivid were his descriptions and lively his anecdotes.

'We must stop here and rest the horses. I can see fresh water in that small valley and there is sufficient grass to keep them happy.' He swung round in his saddle and pointed. That was all he needed to do for the others to understand.

Jenkins and Smith took care of the beasts; her husband and his brother made themselves comfortable on a flat rock and waited for her to prepare them something to eat. She did so with good grace. She could hardly expect either of them to wait on her.

They moved on an hour later and continued in their leisurely way. Jenkins frequently rode on ahead, or dismounted and scrambled up the nearest hill to check they were alone on the track. Twice they saw a donkey loaded down with panniers travelling along the main route, which occasionally they could see from the little used track they were on.

Their party was now riding single file and in silence. Occasionally she saw an eagle or a hawk diving for prey. She loved the mountains. She was going to miss this wild and beautiful countryside when she was living in flat and boring England.

They didn't make camp until dusk. She was an excellent horsewoman and could spend all day in the saddle without coming to grief. From the winces and groans she heard coming from Smith and Jenkins, they were not so lucky. Riflemen travelled with the infantry on foot; they must be less used to riding than the rest of them.

* * *

Perry had instructed Smith to prepare the meal. Sofia had been willing to feed all of them at lunchtime, but it wasn't fair to ask her to wait on the servants in the evening as well. The fire gave a welcome warmth and soon the smell of roasting meat made his mouth water. Zorro was already earning his keep by fetching them rabbits.

The saddles were used as seats and he was sitting next to her. 'This is an interesting wedding trip, sweetheart, but I promise I shall take you somewhere better once this is over. Is there anywhere you would particularly like to see before we return to England?'

'I would love to go to Seville, Madrid or any Spanish city that is free of the French. I travelled extensively with my father but only in rural areas.'

'I am not sure that will be possible, my love. We need to be at Oporto before bad weather starts or we will not get a ship home. I have no wish to stay here for months.'

She nodded and smiled, but he wasn't convinced by this effort. 'I need to see someone who knows more about my eyes. I fear my vision could deteriorate again without the correct treatment.'

Her expression changed to concern. 'Of course we must go home immediately you have located O'Reilly. We have the rest of our lives to travel. I never had a Season. Do you have a house in Town? Perhaps we could spend some time there so I can visit the theatre, museums and lectures.'

'No balls, parties or routs?'

'I should not say no to any of those, but equally I should not be disappointed if there were none. I'm not like other young ladies. I prefer to be outside, not flirting with a gentleman on the dance floor.'

'If ever I catch you flirting with another gentleman there will be hell to pay, madam. However, you may flirt as much as you like with me.'

They continued to exchange pleasantries and

then Beau, who had been giving them some privacy, strolled over to sit down beside them. 'My men are not used to spending so many hours in the saddle. I sincerely hope we are close to our destination.'

Perry decided it was time to arrange the rugs on the ground to make a rudimentary bed for them both. It would be much warmer curled up together and he was looking forward to holding her in his arms all night for the second time even if they couldn't make love.

Smith was no longer with them. He assumed he had gone to scout the area as they must be within a few miles of their destination. Jenkins dished up a tasty stew and this was washed down by a skin of rough red wine for the gentlemen and coffee for Sofia.

They disappeared in turn to do what was necessary and then the campsite settled down for the night. She didn't object to their sleeping arrangements, in fact seemed pleased she was to share his blanket.

As soon as they were comfortable he turned her to face him and began to kiss her. At first she responded but then stiffened in his arms. 'No, not here. There will be nothing of this sort between us until we are sleeping in the privacy of our own bedchamber, wherever that might be.'

'I wasn't intending to do more than kiss you, my

love, but I shall respect your wishes. I meant to ask you, did you bring your lovely wedding gown or has that been abandoned?'

She sighed and relaxed into his embrace. 'I have it safely in one of my saddle bags along with two other gowns and the necessary underpinnings. I'm hoping I shall have the opportunity to wear it again soon, as it is the most beautiful gown I have ever owned.'

He was disappointed she hadn't said she wished to keep it because it was the one she had got married in, but at least she had brought it with her. He had been thinking about her wish to see a Spanish city. Salamanca was on their route to Oporto and this had been freed from the French vermin after a vicious battle that had taken place just before he had set out on his last mission.

They would stay there for a week or two, so they could replenish their wardrobes and hopefully mix with the highest echelons of Spanish society. The city would still be suffering from having been occupied and then violently liberated, but people were resilient and hopefully he would be able to show her the stunning architecture and cathedral. He thought they had been undamaged during the fight.

It would all depend on his brother's finances. He had no money of his own as he had handed it all to the don. He slept lightly, one ear open for trouble, and heard Smith returning in the middle of the night. He carefully rolled sideways and then tucked Sofia back inside the rugs before getting to his feet.

Beau woke as he stepped over him and without being asked he too wriggled out of his cocoon of blankets and came with him to see what news Smith had brought.

Jenkins had remained alert and on guard, and this gave him pause. He was officially still a soldier and should have taken his turn and not been sleeping like a civilian.

'Have we found them?'

'Yes, my lord, we have. There are no sentries outside the village but I saw movement at three of the windows in the houses. They have men guarding the approach from the road. It'll be impossible to attack from that direction.'

'My intention is not to attack at all if we can avoid it, but to somehow get into the place without being detected, find my man and leave.'

'Don't reckon that's possible, sir. Only a mountain goat could get in from any other direction.'

'Were you able to count the horses and work out how many of them there are?' Beau asked.

'Couldn't get close enough, but it ain't a big place

– no more than a huddle of stone houses. Maybe only a dozen or so – certainly no more.'

'I can get you in if you will allow me to.' Sofia had woken and spoke quietly from behind them. He was about to tell her that she was not going to be involved, when he thought again. She had spent the best part of two years roaming the hills with the partisans and might well know something they didn't.

'Go ahead, sweetheart, what do you suggest?'

'I have something similar to a riding habit that I can put on over these breeches. If I take Marron – he's a faster horse than mine – I can gallop up screaming that I am being pursued by brigands. I shall speak in Spanish, naturally, and they will let me in, not because they wish to help me but because they will be short of women of any sort.'

'Why would you be wandering around legitimately in this remote part of the hills? They might shoot you on sight as a partisan.'

'I haven't thought that far. I'm sure between us we can come up with a credible story. We can't be more than an hour from the main route that leads from one village to the next. There are several small towns and villages dotted about. I could easily have come from one of those.'

'I cannot allow you to put yourself at such risk for a man you've not even met,' Perry said firmly.

'O'Reilly knows you better than I do, has saved your life more than once, so you told me. If Smith and Jenkins position themselves carefully in the hills I'm sure they can protect me if things go badly.'

Beau had been listening to this with interest. 'I applaud your courage, Sofia, but even if you do get in, how is that going to help us as we would now have two hostages instead of one to rescue?'

'If this place is as small as Smith says it is, it would not take me long to locate the six prisoners. If I can speak to one of them and tell them that there's a rescue party outside the village, then I'm sure they will make every effort to escape.'

Perry had heard quite enough of this nonsense. It was pointless to argue as his headstrong young wife would continue to insist she was quite capable of entering the enemy camp and then exiting unharmed along with the six other prisoners.

'We shall discuss this further in the morning. Smith and Jenkins need to sleep; they have not done so yet. I shall stand guard for the next three hours and then you can relieve me, brother.'

Nobody questioned his orders and ten minutes

later the place settled back to silence, leaving him alone with his thoughts, and they were not happy ones. His dog joined him and he thought that perhaps there was no need for a guard as the animal would warn him if anyone was close by.

11

Beau tried to make himself more comfortable without disturbing the others. The novelty of sleeping rough had already worn thin and if he were honest he couldn't wait to return to his pampered life of luxury. Presumably his brother would wake him up when it was his turn to stand guard, so he didn't have to worry about being late for his duty.

Sofia's suggestion that she inveigle her way into the French camp was a good one. As far as he could see it was the only way they had the slightest chance of getting in without being killed or captured, and he wasn't sure which would be worse.

He carried no identification, nor did the others, so how could he convince anyone he was in fact a duke and worth exchanging for a French prisoner, or at the very worst demanding a ransom? The only person who had travelled in these hills with papers was Perry, and they had been false, as they suggested he was a wine merchant. God knows what had happened to those because he certainly didn't have them now.

He had intended to stay awake and try and come up with a solution to their problem, but a day in the saddle was enough to send him to sleep despite the discomfort of being stretched out on stony ground with only a blanket to roll up in.

He had barely closed his eyes when he was shaken roughly awake. 'Your turn, Beau. I need to get a few hours' sleep. Wake Jenkins and Smith at dawn but tell them not to light a fire. We shall have to break our fast with yesterday's bread and cheese.'

'Have you come up with a way of effecting the rescue?'

'I think I have. I'll discuss it with you all in the morning.'

This conversation had been conducted in whispers whilst Perry wriggled into the blankets with his wife. Beau was certain his brother was asleep as soon as his head rested on the saddle bag that was being utilised as a pillow.

He took his position in a cleft in the rock where he

could see up onto the track but not be seen himself. One thing he was certain of, Perry wouldn't agree to leave until O'Reilly was free or dead. Beau rather feared it would be the latter and it wouldn't just be the Irishman who perished.

As he huddled into his thick coat, he mulled over the idea that Sofia was to be used as a Trojan horse. It could just work if she could somehow smuggle weapons in with her – otherwise he rather thought it was doomed to failure. A knot formed in the pit of his stomach at the thought of what could happen to his sister-in-law at the hands of her captors. He would rather die than have her suffer in that way.

The hours passed slowly and he was relieved when the first flicker of dawn crept over the horizon. He slid out of his hiding place and went to wake his two men. He warned them about the fire and they nodded. The horses had been hobbled a little further down where there was better grazing and the two men went to fetch them back to the campsite.

'Perry, Sofia, it is time to rise.'

His brother was instantly awake and nodded. Beau hastily moved away to allow them a few moments' privacy before they had to face the horrors of the day. He rolled up his blanket, collected his possessions and replaced them in the saddle bag, and then picked up the saddle and carried it over to where the horses were now standing patiently. They looked as dejected as he felt.

Billy, the huge gelding he had brought for Perry, tried to take a lump out of him as he walked past, and he smacked him on the nose. Sylvester, his own stallion, greeted him with affection. They were both magnificent beasts and worth a small fortune, especially in Spain where good horseflesh was hard to come by. So many were killed in the battles, and then eaten by the hungry soldiers, that neither side found it possible to supplant them with horses of equal worth.

The other two arrived at his side with their own saddles and belongings. 'Perry, I have come up with an idea that might work. Do you think we could barter our horses for O'Reilly? I would think that these two must be worth more to this French company than one Irishman.'

'They might well agree, but then would come after us and take the other three as well once they knew we had them. Also, it would mean someone would have to ride double and I think it highly unlikely any of the mounts we would be left with could get us to safety without collapsing first.'

'Then what do you suggest? Last night you said you had come up with a plan.'

Sofia was busy tearing chunks off the loaf and dividing the cheese into portions. Jenkins had filled an empty wineskin with fresh water, which they all shared. Before they left they would all have to refill their own canteens at the stream.

'We shall eat first and then I'll tell you what we are going to do.'

Beau had to hide his annoyance at being given orders by his younger brother. He was used to being the one in charge and was finding it difficult to be the least important member of this group. Even Sofia was better equipped than he was to participate in a daring rescue.

After their inadequate breakfast they saddled their horses and then Perry deigned to share his thoughts.

'I hate to say it, but the only way we have the slightest chance of success is to go with Sofia's idea. She has sewn two knives into her petticoats and also has her own stiletto secreted in her boot. Not much against so many opponents, but it might be enough.'

'I am prepared to take the chance. All I have to do is hand my weapons to the prisoners and leave the rest to them. Remember, Beau, they are not incarcerated, but working as servants and will be free to wander about the place doing their jobs.'

'For God's sake, both of you, you have not thought this through. Sending a beautiful young woman into a camp full of men will give but one result. They will have only one thing on their minds. The first thing they will see when they toss her onto her back will be the knives hidden in her petticoats.' This was blunt speaking and his brother clenched his fist and he braced himself for the punch. It didn't come. The group was silent and he pressed home his point with even more passion.

'I must speak what I feel. I do not think that the possibility of sacrificing your wife in order to save your orderly is acceptable. Do you not value her as highly as O'Reilly?'

Beau's words were heartfelt. He couldn't understand why Perry was so set on retrieving this person at the risk of all their lives.

The four of them were staring at him as if he had been speaking in tongues but then Jenkins coughed and cleared his throat. 'Forgive me for speaking out of turn, sir, but I reckon his grace is right. O'Reilly won't want to be the cause of hurt to your wife. He'd rather stay where he is. At least he's alive.'

The matter hung in the balance and then his brother said something extremely impolite and turned to stare into the distance. His stance was rigid.

Nobody spoke. They waited for Perry to make his decision.

It was now full light and their faces were clearly visible, whereas before they had been indistinct. When his brother eventually turned it was as if he had aged ten years. He reached out and pulled Sofia into his arms.

'What was I thinking? I have been blinded by my own stupidity. Thank God you had the sense to speak what I should have realised for myself. This is a fool's errand. Sofia, my love, will you ever forgive me?'

She buried her head in his shoulder but didn't answer. Beau gestured to the other two that they move away to allow the young couple some privacy. He sent up a prayer of thankfulness that he had spoken out and not let this mission go any further. Now they could turn around and start making the long journey to Oporto and then back to England and Silchester Court.

Gallivanting about the place was all very well when the weather was warm. Winter came early here and soon the snow would start. They needed to be well away from the hills before that happened. At least on the plains it would be warm and there would be hostelries to stay in overnight. If he never slept on the ground again he would be a happy man.

* * *

Sofia rarely cried, but the relief that Perry had finally seen the folly of this mission was overwhelming. Beau should have spoken up sooner and saved them all a deal of discomfort and worry. The same thing had niggled at the back of her mind, that they shouldn't be risking their lives for someone they didn't know, but she had kept these thoughts at bay until they had been spoken aloud.

'Hush, sweetheart, I can't bear to hear you cry. I should be horsewhipped for bringing you into danger. I should have been taking you on your honeymoon, spoiling you, not asking you to risk being violated in the worst possible way – and why? Your life is far more precious to me than his ever could be and it took my brother to bring me to my senses.'

She sniffed and wiped her nose on his jacket before looking up at him. 'My love, until last night you had no idea any of us would be in such danger. You would have come to the same conclusion...'

'I don't think that I would; that is what terrifies me. Good God, I helped you to sew the knives in your skirt. I should have understood the enormity of what I was asking you to do then, and not have had to be told by my brother.'

'It doesn't matter now. I shan't hold it against you. The French will be driven from the hills very soon and I'm sure that your man will find a way to escape when that happens.'

'I should never have come here. We should have set out straight away for England.'

'Actually, the longer we are wandering about the countryside the better I shall like it. I am rather dreading having to become Lady Peregrine. I don't feel that I shall be very good at it.'

He kissed her fiercely and she responded. His horse prevented things from progressing by attempting to sink his teeth into her husband's shoulder. Perry swore at the animal and Billy put his ears back and had another go, equally unsuccessfully.

With a light heart she was tossed into the saddle and they began the long, slow journey to her new life. It wasn't until they stopped for luncheon that she had another opportunity to speak to him.

'Darling girl, we shall be remaining in Salamanca for a few weeks. It is a beautiful city and was liberated from the French some months ago and should now be recovering from the occupation. Neither of us have sufficient garments; we shall have fresh ones made when we get there. I intend to take you to the grandest ball I can find and you must wear your wedding dress for me.'

'I think that your brother wishes to return as speedily as possible...'

'He will be perfectly content to remain in Salamanca if we can find luxurious accommodation for our stay. I shall also hire a carriage so you can travel in style. If we are to have a trunk full of new clothes then we can hardly continue on horseback.' He pushed a strand of hair from her eyes. 'I intend to be the best husband I can. I shall spoil you, give in to your most extravagant demands. I love you, sweetheart.'

Somehow she hid her dismay; he believed he was giving her something she really wanted. The thought of being obliged to travel several hundred miles in a closed carriage filled her with horror. She was equally unhappy about the thought of being pampered and spoilt – she just wasn't that sort of girl. 'And I shall be the best wife that I can. I love you too and cannot wait to reach Salamanca so I can be your true wife.'

* * *

It took them almost two weeks to reach this city. Zorro and herself were the only members of the group that were disappointed to see it. She would have liked the journey to continue for several weeks more but everyone else in their small party, including the equines, seemed relieved to be there. Jenkins had gone ahead the day before to find them the best lodgings he could.

He met them at the city gates. 'I've rented a grand house for you, your grace; cost a fair bit, mind, but I reckon it's worth every penny. Follow me and I'll take you there.'

Everywhere Sofia looked there was another wonder to behold. The magnificent buildings glowed orange in the sunlight. The ravages of the battles that had taken place a few months ago had mostly been removed.

Elegant women in dark gowns and lace headdresses glided about the place followed by their servants carrying baskets full of interesting items. The gentlemen, their black hair oiled back, walked together in their black suits and snowy white shirts.

'The *Plaza Mayor* is no more than a hundred yards from the house that I rented, my lord. I've never seen the like, and I've travelled most places on the continent,' Jenkins said.

The house proved to be everything he had said and more. The occupiers had perished in the battle and the owners were delighted to have rich English aristocracy stay there at an exorbitant rent. It was fully staffed and was the most luxurious building she had ever set foot in.

The major-domo conducted them to their apartments. Beau had been given the most palatial, as was only right as he was the Duke of Silchester, but the accommodation she and Perry had was almost as wonderful.

'The first thing I want is a bath. I shall send for hot water immediately.'

'No need to do that, sweetheart. See here, we have a joint sitting room and matching bedchambers and dressing rooms. There is already a bath ready and waiting for each of us.'

He kissed her hard and her pulse skittered. Would he suggest they tumble into bed before they went downstairs? She had thought she could stay away from him, possibly have the marriage annulled, but that was foolish thinking. He was her husband and she his wife. They had promised they would be the best they could be and she, for one, would not go back on her word.

Her ability to converse in their native tongue with the two maids allocated to her made things so much easier. Whilst she luxuriated in the rose-scented water the girls had unpacked the saddle bags and one of them had run off to press her three gowns.

Her fingers were wrinkled by the time she stepped out into the waiting, warmed towels. She could hear male voices from the sitting room so guessed that Beau had joined her husband. She was tardy, but had no intention of hurrying. She was far too relaxed after her long immersion in the water.

Her hair still had to be redressed and that would take some time as there was so much of it. Without thinking she raised her voice. 'Perry, I shall be another half an hour. I will join you downstairs when I am ready.'

The bedchamber door opened and he strolled in. Apart from a clean shirt and freshly tied neckcloth, he looked no different than he had before. He still had on his riding clothes. She was about to comment but then understood he had nothing else as their limited luggage had been given over to her.

'My love, there are servants who can take messages. There is no necessity for you to yell in order to bring me to your side.'

'Fiddlesticks to that! I was going to have my hair arranged elaborately but I don't think I will bother.' She spoke rapidly to the girl and it took just a few moments for her long plait to be curled around her head and pinned in place.

'There, I am ready. I cannot wait to explore this beautiful city. We have ample time as dinner will not be served until nine o'clock.'

He took her hand and kissed her knuckle. 'Dinner will be served at whatever time we decide is convenient to us.'

'Then we are eating before we go out?'

'No, my brother and I have decided we rather like eating late, so today at least we shall dine in the dark. Come along, sweetheart, I want to show you around this grand house before we promenade around the square.'

There were some further half a dozen bedchambers on this floor, and servants' quarters and the nursery floors above. Everywhere was immaculate, a little ornate for her taste, but one had to admire the abundance of gold on everything.

'This is the most impressive room, my love, and I wish to keep it until last,' Perry said as he pushed open huge double doors with a flourish.

'A ballroom – it's absolutely stunning. See how high the ceilings are? Look at the murals, the marble pillars. I've never seen anything quite so beautiful.'

She ran from one delight to the next exclaiming in amazement.

She turned to see her husband and brother-in-law watching her. Their smiles were indulgent as if she were a child at a party and not a woman grown. Her pleasure trickled away to be replaced by annoyance. If they thought her childish then she would behave as they expected.

She clapped her hands as if she were a silly debutante. 'We must have a ball here before we leave. I can wear my wedding gown. You must both arrange for evening dress, as well as the other things you need, to be made for you.' She smiled brightly and the two men exchanged glances.

'There is nothing I should like better, my love, than to hold a ball here so we can celebrate our marriage in style. However, as we have only just arrived and know no one to invite, I think...'

'We have the Duke of Silchester in our party. I am certain that his name on an invitation will bring all the prestigious families flocking to meet you. The Spaniards love a party, and especially a spontaneous one.'

She tilted her head in what she hoped was a coquettish way. She was rather enjoying this playacting as both gentlemen were looking more and more bewildered by her behaviour.

'I shall understand, your grace, if it is because of the cost of such an event that you hesitate. I know that my husband has no funds, and I certainly brought none to this marriage.'

It wasn't done to speak of such a vulgar thing as money, as she very well knew, and to suggest that her husband was totally dependent on his brother for everything would put the cat amongst the pigeons.

'If you are determined on this, my dear, then I shall be delighted to set things in motion,' Beau said through gritted teeth. Perry was staring at her through narrowed eyes and she wished she had not started this masquerade.

She picked up her skirt and curtsied as if to the king himself. Then laughed at their expressions. 'I was jesting. I am not such a ninnyhammer as to demand such a thing. I do apologise if you thought me serious.'

The duke laughed. 'I'm glad to hear that, Sofia. I was beginning to think that the sun had addled your wits.'

Perry took her arm and his grip was firm enough to make his anger clear. 'Forgive me, brother, I need to speak to my wife in private. We shall join you shortly.'

She wanted to call Beau back but his long strides took him from the ballroom before she had time to do so.

'Let go of my arm, Perry; you are hurting me.'

Instantly she was released but he did not apologise. 'You will not put on such a display again – is that quite clear? You might have thought you were jesting, but you embarrassed both of us by your poor taste.'

She poked her tongue out at him. 'If you treat me as a child then you can expect childish behaviour. Now, is that all or do you have further things to say to me?'

He tugged her elbows and tumbled her into his arms. 'You are a baggage, but I love you anyway.'

It was some time before they left the ballroom and joined the duke, who one might have expected to be irritated, but he was wandering about examining the murals and paintings as if they hadn't been an unconscionable time.

12

The following day the seamstress arrived with a bevy of helpers to take measurements. It soon became clear to Sofia that they had no idea what she wanted and were determined to make her gowns in the Spanish style.

'Señora, I have changed my mind. I should just like two cotton nightgowns without embellishment, four petticoats and half a dozen pairs of stockings. We are returning home and I shall replenish my gowns when I get there.'

The woman seemed unbothered that she no longer had a big order and promised to have what she wanted delivered later that day. Either she had dozens of girls sewing for her, or these items were already made.

Perry was being measured next door and she knocked and walked in without waiting for his permission. 'I don't want to stay here more than another day or two. I should like to set out as soon as possible for England. I am just having nightwear and underpinnings.'

He looked relieved and told the unfortunate tailor he didn't need jackets and breeches but two shirts and some more stockings. These were also going to be delivered that afternoon.

'I cannot tell you how relieved I am, sweetheart, not to have to remain here for several weeks. I would do so if that is what you want, but as you don't, I am delighted.' He held out his arms and she ran into them.

'Have I told you today how much I love you?'

'Once or twice, but I think your actions last night were enough to convince me of your devotion.'

His arms tightened and his eyes blazed. She was rather enjoying being a married lady after all. 'Do you think I could already be increasing? I would really like to be settled before that happens.'

His laugh was deep and sent her pulse skittering. 'It is quite possible, darling girl, that you were increasing before we were married. You must know when you had your last monthly courses.'

'This is a strange conversation to be having, but they have never been regular and I have no notion how long it is since the last one. They can be as far apart as two months sometimes.'

'In which case we are none the wiser. Shall we give Beau the good news? He has gone out to find someone who will deliver the letter to your mother that you wrote last night. He has also let the family know that I am well, married, and will be returning shortly.'

'I have one request to make, my love, and you will think it quite ridiculous.'

He raised an eyebrow and she giggled. 'I stand in fear and trepidation to hear what it might be.'

'I am going to wear my wedding dress tonight and I wish to dance with you in the ballroom; imagine that I am at a grand party. It is quite likely that by the time I am able to attend my first ball I might well be in an interesting condition and unable to do so.'

He kissed her and shook his head. 'That is a contradiction, sweetheart, but I know what you mean. I will certainly dance with you tonight. I shall ask them to serve dinner in the dining room with as much ceremony as they can muster.'

'Good heavens, please do not do that. Things are quite formal enough without asking them to fuss even more.'

The duke returned, having been successful in his mission, and was even more thrilled than Perry had been to hear they were to return almost immediately.

'Jenkins and Smith have yet to locate a carriage.'

'I am perfectly content to continue to ride, in fact I would prefer to do so. Now we are not to have a trunk full of new garments there is no necessity for the carriage, is there?'

He nodded solemnly and his expression was amused. 'I cannot argue with your logic, my dear. Are you happy to leave tomorrow?'

'I am indeed. I do hope you can get a refund on the rent...' She stopped and clapped her hands on her mouth as if she was trying to push the words back. She looked at her husband, expecting him to be angry, but he exchanged a look with his brother and they both started to laugh.

When they were finally silent she was able to speak without setting them off again. 'As you found my question so amusing, your grace, perhaps you would deign to answer it?'

'It is none of your business, young lady, but as you insist on knowing I shall tell you the arrangement is on a day-to-day basis. I will inform the major-domo we are leaving tomorrow and then settle the account.'

They ambled around the stunning city but she was relieved when they returned to the house shortly after midday. 'I am going to rest, gentlemen. I shall see you at dinner.'

* * *

Tonight she didn't care if her escorts had no evening rig. She intended to look as beautiful as she could. The two maids were delighted to be asked to arrange her hair in an elaborate style. She had no jewellery, but the gown was so elegant it required nothing further. There was a full-length glass in the dressing room and she admired herself from every angle.

The new petticoats and silk stockings had arrived earlier than expected and so she would not be obliged to go down in bare feet as she had the night before. She had thought Perry might disturb her nap, but he had not come into her room. In fact, she had no idea what he had been doing with himself for the remainder of the day.

'There, my lady, you look like a princess. So beautiful with your English hair and eyes,' one of the maids said. As Sofia's hair was dark and her eyes hazel she hardly thought she was the typical English rose but did not bother to argue.

'Make sure that all my belongings are packed in the saddle bags ready for us to leave first thing.' She indicated what she would be wearing the next day and they were shocked that she would be wearing men's attire. 'I shall pack this ensemble myself when I retire. I shall not need you again and I thank you for your assistance these past two days.'

Perry tapped on the door and walked in. There was no need to ask him if he approved; his expression said it all. 'You are the most beautiful woman in Christendom and I am the luckiest man. Take my arm, my love, and I shall take you down to dinner.'

'You have had your hair cut, and that is a new shirt you are wearing.'

'Do you like the new look?'

'It suits you short – but then it suited you long as well. In fact, husband, you would be handsome wearing sackcloth and ashes.'

She slipped her hand through his arm, loving the feel of his muscles beneath her fingers. There was something about him tonight, something she couldn't put her finger on. She glanced sideways at him and he smiled his wicked smile, making her forget everything else.

Beau looked magnificent as usual. They might not be wearing evening pantaloons but their boots were polished to a high shine, their topcoats immaculate, and both had frothy white neckcloths above handsome silk waistcoats.

'You have both purchased new waistcoats as well as stocks – did you go out for them whilst I was asleep?'

'No, they were delivered with our shirts and things. I thought we could eat *al fresco* as the evening is so clement.'

* * *

The dinner was sumptuous, the champagne cold, but he scarcely noticed what he put in his mouth. He had a surprise for his beautiful young wife and he couldn't wait to show her.

When the final plate was cleared he stood up and held out his hand. 'Will you dance with me, my lady?'

Her smile was radiant. 'I should be honoured, my lord.'

She slipped her gloved hand into his and he pulled it through his arm. He led her back into the house and as planned the sound of a string quartet drifted through the house.

The look she gave him made the effort he had put into this worthwhile. She released his arm and grabbed his hand; by the time they reached the ballroom they were both running. He could hear his brother laughing behind them.

The musicians continued to play for a few moments and then paused. He nodded and the beautiful sound of a waltz swirled around the room.

She curtsied, he bowed, and then he swept her away. All Wellington's officers were expected to dance superbly and he was no exception. By the time the last notes faded, instead of being at arm's length she was crushed against his chest.

'Thank you, thank you, darling Perry. That was the most magical experience. How many times will you dance with me?'

'As many as you want, sweetheart, but you must partner my brother at least once or he will be disappointed. You are the most beautiful girl here tonight.'

She giggled and he loved her even more, if that were possible. After their third waltz Beau was waiting for his turn.

'I think this is going to be a country dance, your grace.' She said this with a commendably straight face and his brother replied as if this were a sensible suggestion.

'Then we shall lead the set, my lady. It is some time since I have danced, so you will forgive me if I do not live up to your expectations.'

The quartet played the opening chords of another waltz and Beau swept her away. Perry moved to the side to watch them, or rather to watch her. His brother rarely danced but he was light on his feet and they made a pretty couple.

She was laughing at something he said and for a second he wanted to snatch her away, to not allow her to dance with anyone else but him. He had not thought himself a jealous man, and especially not of his brother, but she was his world and he wasn't prepared to share her with anyone.

His first task when they returned would be to get his siblings involved in finding the duke a bride. He didn't for one minute think Beau would do anything untoward, but he was a dangerously attractive man and it would be safer for everyone if he was married.

No sooner had he thought this than he was ashamed. How could he consider for one second that his beloved Sofia might fall in love with another man? The dance drew to a close and he indicated to the musicians that they could go. The hour was late and they were intending to leave at first light and all needed to get some sleep. He sincerely hoped that he and his wife would have considerably less sleep than his brother.

'I shall never forget tonight,' she said and ran to the end of the ballroom where she twirled and curtsied to them both before dancing back. 'This will always be my favourite gown and I intend to wear it so often that you will be sick of the sight of it.'

He gathered her close and with his arm firmly around her waist guided her upstairs to their palatial apartment. 'A lady of the *ton* would rather die than be seen in the same gown on consecutive occasions. You will have a new wardrobe and half a dozen ballgowns to choose from.'

She looked at him in astonishment. 'I shall wear what I like; I will not be dictated to by anyone. I have no intention of allowing you to buy me dozens of unnecessary gowns. I would prefer you to give the money to those who are struggling to put food on the table.'

'I had not known you were a revolutionary, sweetheart. Whatever your wishes on the matter you are now a member of the Sheldon family and must dress appropriately.'

She didn't respond but when they walked into their apartment she slipped from his grasp. 'It is late, Perry. We both need to get as much sleep as possible before our long journey. Goodnight, thank you for a wonderful evening. I shall see you in the morning.'

The door to her bedchamber was closed firmly behind her. He could demand his conjugal rights, but that wasn't his way. Once she had met his sisters she would understand what was expected of her so there was no point in being at daggers drawn when they were still so far from home.

* * *

The journey to the coast was uneventful. It would have been more enjoyable if he had been able to share a bed with his beloved. He enjoyed her company during the day – she was as amusing, argumentative and adorable as always – but every night she had some objection to them making love and he respected her wishes. His dog appeared to have changed allegiance now he was no longer needed as a guide. He spent every available minute at Sofia's side and he was glad she had someone of her own.

He observed his brother becoming captivated as the days went past. The more he saw them together, the more concerned he became. He was pleased they were good friends but wished they did not laugh so much. Indeed, if he was honest, Sofia was more animated in Beau's company than she was in his.

It was with some relief that they finally reached the port and were able to board the waiting ship that would take them back to England. He had been away for over two years and so much had happened in his absence. Aubrey had got married, so had Giselle and there had been several babies born.

'I shall share with you, Beau, and let Sofia have the cabin to herself. We might be needed to help with the horses.' His brother didn't argue. 'Smith and Jenkins are going to sleep with the animals – I gather none of them enjoyed the crossing last time.'

'We must pray it will be calm. The weather is remarkably clement for October, but we have a long way to go and storms can appear out of nowhere.'

'It would be ironic, indeed, if after you have sent the good news of my return we all perished in the sea.'

'Tarnation take it! What the hell is the matter with you, little brother? You have a face as long as a wheelbarrow most of the time. One would have thought you would be overjoyed to be going back with a beautiful young wife on your arm. Yet you have been a veritable curmudgeon the entire journey.'

'Things are not going smoothly between us. I fear

that Sofia will not settle into her new life. She has been running wild in the hills for these past two years doing God knows what, and now we expect her to behave like a young girl with no experience of the world.'

His brother slapped him none too gently on the shoulder. 'Do not include me in that sentence, Perry. Sofia is no different from our sisters apart from the fact that she has no interest in fashion. She will find her way. Give her time; do not hedge her in with etiquette and protocol.'

This was an astounding thing for him to hear. His brother was an aristocrat, a duke, from his crown to his toes, and expected everybody to treat him with deference and obey him to the letter. How could Beau have changed so radically? He scarcely recognised him as the brother he had left behind when he had joined the cavalry.

As it happened, all four of them were needed to keep the horses from breaking free. Even if he had wanted to spend time with Sofia he wouldn't have been able to in the circumstances. He could not understand why his twin had chosen to spend the first year of his marriage on the sea. It was a hideous place to be – wet, cold and dangerously uncomfortable. Perry vowed he would never set foot in another ship as long as he lived. It was a good thing he hadn't suggested to his wife that they take the yacht themselves when Aubrey and Mary returned from their travelling.

'I am hoping that the letter I sent will have reached Silchester in time for my instructions to be followed. I asked for rooms to be booked for the night and our valets, and a maid for Sofia, to be waiting with fresh garments. The carriage should also be there and a fresh team left at a posting station so we can make the journey without being obliged to overnight a second time.'

'I intended to travel inside with my wife so we can have an opportunity to talk. Will the servants return by common stage?'

'They will return in the same manner that they arrived. In the second coach.'

Perry wondered what his wife would think about such unnecessary expenditure. The cost of this enterprise would keep half the population of the town she had been living in for six months. Even before she had lived so simply in Spain, she had not come from a wealthy family.

Bennett, second in line to Beau, had married the daughter of a cit – but she had been fabulously wealthy. Madeline had married an ex-soldier who had recently inherited the title – but he also was comfortably off. Aubrey had married a widow a few years older than himself – but again she was from an excellent family and wealthy in her own right. Finally, his younger sister Giselle had married a man much older than herself, Lord Rushton, Beau's closest friend.

He had married a girl with little connection to society, no experience of moving in the best circles and no money of her own. She had intelligence, courage, beauty and compassion – what she didn't have was the upbringing and training that would make her life easier.

PART II

ENGLAND

13

Sofia accepted the ministrations of her new maid reluctantly. She was perfectly capable of dressing and undressing herself, but she must accept this was how things were going to be in future. Falling in love with a blind man with no identity was quite different from being married to the brother of the Duke of Silchester.

'There you are, my lady; that ensemble is perfect for you. Cherry red complements your colouring. Shall I tie the bonnet ribbons or will you wait until after you have broken your fast to put it on?'

'I have eaten sufficient, Polly, so I might as well be ready to leave when the gentlemen come down.'

The bonnet was lined with the same red material

that edged the gown and pelisse. Even her gloves were dyed to match – she felt quite ridiculous and longed to be able to put on the breeches and shirts that she had been wearing for the past few years.

Something occurred to her. 'Make sure the items I was wearing when I arrived have been packed.'

The girl looked shifty. 'His lordship instructed me to throw them out, my lady, and they...'

This was the outside of enough. 'You are my dresser; you will follow my instructions. Do I make myself clear? If you wish to retain your position you had better remember this. Whatever you have done with them you will find them and pack them or you will be dismissed without reference.'

The girl gulped and ran off. Sofia knew she was being unfair but Perry had had no right to dispose of her personal possessions in this high-handed way. She prayed Polly would find them as she had no wish to punish her maid for her husband's sins.

There was no sign of the luxurious carriage, which bore the Silchester arms, outside so she thought she would go and look at the sea. Viewing it from the land was preferable to being on it. As she was exiting the hostelry it belatedly occurred to her that she really should not be wandering about the place without an escort of some sort. Zorro, as always, was waiting to accompany her wherever she went. He had adjusted well to his new circumstances and appeared unbothered at being obliged to sleep in the stables.

Then she spotted Jenkins. He would be ideal. She waited in the doorway until he looked her way and then beckoned him over.

'Good morning, my lady, is there something I can do for you?'

'I should like to go for a walk before I am obliged to sit in a stuffy carriage for hours. I wish you to accompany me.'

He looked over her shoulder as if expecting to see Perry behind her. Then she realised he was looking for her maid. 'It's all very confusing. Will I be breaking some unwritten rule if I take a walk with only you as my escort?'

He scratched his head. 'I ain't sure, but there's no one here to complain. There's a path that leads to the cliffs and I reckon we could go along there as long as we ain't too long. His grace sent word to the stables to be ready to leave in an hour.'

The walk was exactly what she wanted and she returned feeling that the brisk sea breeze had blown away her worries. They walked back into the inn's yard to see the carriage, with its two matching bays stamping impatiently in the traces, waiting to depart. There was no sign of either the duke or Perry so she got Jenkins to let down the steps and she climbed inside. The squabs were of leather and soft beneath her touch. This was luxury indeed and it might not be quite so unpleasant travelling in here after all.

She hadn't slept well despite the comfort of her bed and she dozed off, ignoring the raised voices and running feet she could hear outside. Then the carriage tilted violently and Perry joined her inside.

'Have you any idea of the trouble you've caused? Dammit, Sofia, we've been searching for you this past hour. Did it not occur to you that getting into the carriage without telling anyone was a stupid thing to do?'

His abrupt arrival and furious words jerked her rudely from her sleep. He was no more than an arm's length from her. His cheeks were flushed and his eyes arctic.

She yawned in his face, stretched slowly and then deigned to answer. 'It is hardly my fault, my lord, if you are so *stupid* that you did not think to speak to Jenkins as to my whereabouts. I do hope you do not intend to travel inside with me, for I have no wish to share this cramped space with a gentleman I no longer recognise as the man I saved from certain death a few months ago.'

His jaw tightened and she could almost hear his teeth grind as he fought to hold on to his temper. Then he retreated as suddenly as he had arrived, kicked the steps up and slammed the door.

She wished the words unsaid. He had probably been worried about her absence and had not thought to ask Jenkins. Why should he think this man would know her whereabouts? Her hands stopped shaking and she stood up intending to go in search of him and apologise.

As she did so the carriage jolted forward, she lost her footing and fell against the door. It flew open she tumbled head first onto the cobbles.

* * *

Perry was about to mount his horse when to his horror his wife fell from the carriage and sprawled face down on the ground. He was beside her in a second, his fury forgotten. He stiffened as Zorro snarled behind him.

'Sweetheart, stay still for a minute whilst I check you have broken no limbs.'

She stirred beneath his touch and rolled over without his assistance. 'I am perfectly well, thank you, Perry. I am merely embarrassed. Would you be so kind as to assist me to my feet?' She reached around and patted the dog who immediately relaxed.

There were dirt smudges on her cheeks, her bonnet was askew, and there were tears in her eyes. He scooped her up and as his brother approached he shook his head. 'If you are sure you are unhurt, darling girl, then allow me to replace you in the carriage. I sincerely hope you do not emerge so precipitously a second time.'

His teasing words had the desired effect as she managed a watery smile. 'You are ridiculous...'

'If you say so, my love, then I must be.' He ducked and climbed in without the benefit of the steps and twisted so he could sit whilst keeping her in his arms. The under-coachman peered nervously into the carriage and then hastily closed the door.

Perry carefully undid the ribbons of her bonnet and tossed it onto the opposite squab. Then he pulled off his gloves using his teeth and they joined the bonnet on the seat. She had remained silent and passive in his arms whilst he did so.

He rubbed the tears and dirt streaks from her face with his handkerchief. 'To continue, sweetheart, I believe that I am also stupid and ungrateful. Have I omitted anything on this list of my sins?'

She sighed and finally relaxed into his embrace. 'I

am sorry that I caused you so much upset. I just went for a walk. I was angry because you had told Polly to throw away my men's garments and I needed to clear my head. Jenkins was my escort.'

He kissed her lightly and she didn't recoil, which was a good sign. 'Is that all? You must realise, Sofia, that your days of riding astride dressed like a boy have gone. I have no objection to you riding astride as long as you remain on Silchester land and do not go abroad. I am sure a garment can be constructed that will make this possible and not send shockwaves through the family.'

The carriage had trundled out of the yard and was now making slow progress through the press of other vehicles along the narrow streets of Dover. They wouldn't be stopping until it was time to change the horses. He must assume that Jenkins or Smith was now leading Billy.

She wriggled off his lap and while still holding on to his arms relocated to the other side of the carriage. For a moment he thought it was because she didn't wish to sit next to him but then she explained why she had moved.

'I need to be able to see your face when we talk and I cannot do so unless I sit opposite. There has been a distance between us since we left Salamanca and we need to address this before we reach Silchester.'

He pushed out his legs and trapped hers between them. He wanted to be in physical contact with her whilst she spoke, as he had a feeling he was going to hear things he didn't want to know. Hopefully, the physical attraction between them would be enough to prevent them from becoming permanently estranged.

'Do I have your permission to speak frankly?'

He flinched. Had it come to that? Did she really think things had changed so much between them that she needed to have his permission before speaking?

'Go ahead, sweetheart. I give you my word I shall not interrupt until you are done.'

She closed her eyes as if gathering her thoughts. She pushed herself more upright on the squabs, and then began. 'I'm beginning to fear that we have made the most catastrophic error by becoming man and wife. I am not denying that we are in love with each other, but I have finally understood that love does not conquer all.

'We are as different as chalk and cheese. Tell me honestly, Perry, if I had not so foolishly come to your house that night would we be married now?'

'I don't know – possibly not. I do not doubt the love we have for each other, but like you I have been having serious concerns about how we are going to adjust to living together in such different circumstances.'

She glanced down at his legs, making it clear she wished to be free of them and obediently he swung them to one side. This was not going well. Instead of clearing the air it was making things more difficult between them.

'I am not suited to living the restricted life of the pampered wife of an English aristocrat. I have no interest in the things that I should. I have no wish to spend time on pointless morning calls, supper parties and musical evenings. I do not play the pianoforte, paint pretty watercolours or do embroidery.

'Nevertheless, I shall do my best to adapt to my new circumstances. I pray that we have a large family, as I believe that is something I should enjoy. I sincerely hope that we don't live to regret our impulsive decision.'

Tears were trickling down her cheeks but she raised a hand when he went to offer her comfort. There was nothing he could say that would make things better. Marrying her and bringing her to England was like putting a wildcat in a cage.

'I love you; do not doubt that for a minute, sweetheart. I would give my life for you. I would kill anyone who harmed a hair on your head, but everything you say is correct. I too will do my best to make things easy for you, to allow you as much freedom as I can.'

He reached out and pulled down both window blinds in turn. Then, ignoring her slight protest, he pulled her almost roughly onto his lap. 'What we do have, darling, is this.'

He had never made love in a moving carriage but it was exactly what they needed to heal the rift between. The danger of discovery, the hilarity of being rocked and bounced from place to place, renewed the one thing they shared. They had passion and he intended that this flame continued to burn and prayed that it would be enough to see them through the difficult times that were coming.

* * *

After tumbling into the well of the carriage twice she and Perry remained there. It was cramped and uncomfortable but the most exciting thing she had ever done. The thought that at any moment the carriage might stop, or the duke might bang on the window demanding to speak to her husband, just made it all the more thrilling.

When it was over and they had rearranged their

clothes, they were both flushed and breathless. He pulled her onto his lap and kissed her with a thoroughness that made her wish they were somewhere they could continue this to its delicious conclusion once again.

'I must apologise...' he began.

'You must not. We are a married couple and can do as we please. I am quite sure we are not the first to behave as we just did in a moving vehicle. A thoroughly exhilarating experience, my lord, even if you did have your boots on.'

His laugh sent shivers down her spine but fortunately the carriage began to slow. They must be approaching the inn where the horses could be exchanged for the second team. When Jenkins had explained, she had been part horrified at the extravagance and part impressed by the efficiency.

'Where is my bonnet? I cannot get out so dishevelled; it will be immediately obvious what we have been doing. I shall die of mortification if your brother was to see us like this. He is a stickler for the rules. He might pretend it is otherwise, but I can sense his disapproval when I misbehave.'

'I'm in no better case than you, sweetheart, so I think we must pretend to be asleep. Quickly, grab the furs from the floor and we shall drape them over us before anyone can look in.'

She was giggling so much she was sure it could be heard outside the vehicle. Eventually they were covered and he put his boots on the opposite squab and then she settled back into his arms with her legs stretched out in front of her.

Her breathing gradually slowed and matched his. It was strangely soporific breathing in and out at the same time as somebody else. Her eyes became heavy just as the carriage turned into the yard. Then as the door was opened she saw her missing bonnet quite squashed in the well of the carriage.

'Perry, my poor bonnet, it is quite ruined.' She covered her mouth to keep back another giggle. He was quivering beneath her, trying to hold back his laughter.

'So it is, my love, how very unfortunate.' His voice was choked. She daren't look at him.

The door was hastily closed, leaving them to laugh until the tears ran down their cheeks. Nobody suggested they got out for refreshments and in a short space of time they were on their way again.

'The carriage has a fresh team. Did your brother and the other two change horses as well?'

'Beau will now be riding Billy. Smith and Jenkins

will remain here until their horses are rested and they can continue. They will be bringing Sylvester and the carriage horses with them when they return, but probably not until tomorrow.'

It was stifling under the rugs and she tossed them aside and put her feet to the floor of the carriage. 'I am looking forward to meeting your family, and your nieces and nephews. Do you think we will arrive in time for me to be introduced today?'

'I think it might be better, sweetheart, if we left it until tomorrow. In fact, I sincerely hope they haven't formed a welcome party.'

'Now that you mention it, I am sure that they have. After all you are rather like the prodigal son...'

He snorted and flicked her cheek with his finger. 'I am nothing like...' Then he stopped and she saw his expression change as he reconsidered. 'I have certainly come back penniless, have behaved in a reprehensible way, but I don't believe the person in the Bible story brought back the greatest gift of all – a wife.'

'This is going to be an unmitigated disaster, Perry, for both of us, especially for me. My bonnet is past redemption and my gown is little better.'

He didn't answer but dropped the window – the blinds were already rolled back where they should be

– and stuck his head out. His brother appeared along-side. 'How far behind us is the carriage with our ser-vants and garments?'

The duke moved away and then returned. 'Not in hailing distance; that's for sure.'

'In which case you must ride ahead and make sure there is no reception committee. We are both in disarray from the journey and I wish to introduce my wife when she is happy with her appearance.'

Beau ducked his head so he could see her and, to her astonishment, he winked. 'It shall be done, little brother. The joyous reunion can take place tomorrow morning. Actually, that makes perfect sense as the infants can be there as well if we postpone.'

He vanished and she hugged Perry with relief. 'I cannot think why I am so nervous of your brother half the time and the other half I find him the most convivial company.'

For some reason this comment seemed to please him. 'He has been head of the family for almost ten years and grew up with the expectation of being the Duke of Silchester. It is small wonder he has a high opinion of himself. It is well deserved.'

'Do you think he knows why we are both looking so dishevelled?'

'What makes you think so?'

'He winked at me. Why else would he do something so risqué if he did not know?'

'If he does, then he will be envious rather than disapproving. I don't suppose he has ever done anything so... so unusual in his life. I have been thinking, sweetheart, that once you are settled you must join with me in finding him a bride. I fear that if we do not do so he will be forever interfering in our lives.'

'Good gracious! If he has not chosen to marry, has not even come close, and yet he is already past his prime, I think we must assume he is a confirmed bachelor.' She hesitated, not sure if she should continue on this delicate subject. 'Does he keep a mistress in London whom he visits?'

'How do you know of such things? I hope you are not intending to ask him.'

She was about to protest that she was not so silly and then saw he was having difficulty keeping his face straight. She punched him on his arm. 'Answer my question. The answer is crucial to your plan.'

'He does, or he did, but I've not been in England for a while and things could have changed. There is something you should know about my family. All of us without exception have known within a day or two that we have met the person we wish to marry. Beau has been hunted all his adult life by predatory matrons hoping to foist their daughters onto him. He has learned to stay away from places where he was likely to be pursued.'

'Then it is small wonder he has not been able to find himself a young lady he can love. I shall give the matter some thought. Having a project to complete will provide me with something to do apart from the frivolous nonsense most wives are expected to take part in.'

He moved away from her and the close connection they had forged by their disgraceful behaviour was severed. What had she done to upset him this time?

14

Beau cantered away from the carriage, relieved his brother and his new wife appeared to have settled their differences. He did not doubt their regard for each other, nor did he think for one minute they were not ideally suited – however, he could foresee problems for both of them.

Perry had intended to make his life in the military, become the colonel of a regiment in time, and now he had been forced to resign his commission and return to a life he had found less than satisfying. Being the Duke of Silchester, running the vast estates here and in the north, was not enough for him, so how could he expect his younger brother to be satisfied with so much less?

It was a conundrum and he could see no satisfactory conclusion. He smiled wryly. He had thought that gallivanting off to Spain would satisfy his *ennui*, but it had not. The novelty of being obliged to sleep in the open, live like a peasant, had soon worn off and he was eager to get back to his life.

Bennett, the brother closest to him in age, had also been a soldier, as had Carshalton, the man who had married his eldest sister Madeline, and yet both of them were content in their domestic life. He must discuss the matter with them and ask them how they had adjusted so well.

Sofia was unlike any of his siblings or their spouses, was unused to moving in the highest circles, being expected to behave impeccably at all times, and he doubted she would adjust easily to her new life. God willing, she would soon be increasing and then have infants to occupy her time. This did not solve the problem of his brother. Perry was a man of action and being idle would not suit him.

He had only two small estates to occupy his time – but there were other things he could do. Perhaps his brother could become involved in some business venture. Shipping was a trade but not one that would be considered below the notice of the Sheldon family.

Since receiving the funds from Bennett's marriage

settlement, the family coffers were full. He had invested wisely and he was confident he could give half the money to Perry and Aubrey so they could jointly buy into a commercial venture of some sort.

He had not told his brother that his twin, Aubrey, and his new wife, Mary, had just returned from their travels and were now residing in the newly refurbished east wing of Silchester Court. They were identical in appearance, but different in character. It would be wonderful to have all the family close by again.

Billy ate up the miles and in two hours he was cantering on his own land. His arrival had been seen from the house and a groom was waiting to take the sweating horse. The butler greeted him effusively.

'Welcome home, your grace. The family are waiting to be summoned. How far behind you is Lord Peregrine?'

'Two hours at least. There will be no gathering today. Have messages taken immediately informing my siblings that they are to be here at eleven o'clock tomorrow morning instead.'

Peebles bowed. 'I shall see to it immediately, your grace. Will dinner be required downstairs?'

'No. I shall eat with Lord Aubrey. Inform the

kitchen that trays are to be sent to Lord and Lady Peregrine. Have hot water waiting for them.'

He was on his way to his apartment to change his soiled garments when the estate manager waylaid him. 'Welcome back, your grace, might I be permitted to have a word with you before you go upstairs?'

'Carstairs, I take it this is urgent and cannot wait until tomorrow?'

'I fear not. I have been lurking here all day in the hope of catching you.'

'Come, we shall go to my study.' He snapped his fingers and the footman, waiting to open the door for whichever room he approached, stood to attention. 'Have coffee and bread and cheese sent to us.'

The room was immaculate. He would have been surprised if it was not, but the desk was alarmingly high with documents and letters waiting to be dealt with. Bennett had been tasked with acting as head of the family in his absence, so he was surprised to see so many things awaiting him.

'Sit, Carstairs, and tell me what has agitated you.'

'There has been unrest on your estates in the north and three farms and a manor house have been razed to the ground.'

'When did this happen? Are any of my people injured?'

'No one has been hurt but your tenants and the family leasing the house are homeless. Now that you are back I can travel there and see for myself what is going on.'

Beau gestured to the piles of paper on his desk. 'I thought Lord Sheldon was dealing with all this.'

'Lord Sheldon is not here. He was called to London by the prime minister shortly after you left and has not yet returned.'

'I have only been away two months and yet I have returned to chaos. I am sure that Lady Sheldon will have more information about my brother and I shall ask her when I see her tomorrow. I intend to start on this backlog of paperwork tomorrow. You must travel post-chaise. I need you to be there as soon as possible. Send word by express when you know more. Your first task is to find my tenants somewhere temporary to live.'

His estate manager shared the refreshments whilst they talked of events in the neighbourhood. This was not the homecoming he had envisaged for his younger brother. He had hoped to be able to devote his time to Perry and Sofia, help them to settle in. Now he would have to leave them to their own devices as his estate would need his undivided attention.

* * *

Silchester Court was as magnificent as she feared, not at all the sort of place she was going to feel comfortable in. The closer she got to what was going to be her home for the foreseeable future, the more miserable she was. The fact that Perry remained on the far side of the carriage, his expression shuttered, looking as unhappy as she, did nothing to restore her equanimity.

The carriage didn't pull up with a flourish outside the imposing portico with its marble pillars and elegant steps, but continued around to the back. The steps were let down and they were ushered into the house like unwanted guests.

This must be the duke's doing, and it merely served to reinforce her reservations. For a horrible moment she thought they were also going to have to ascend to their accommodation via the servants' stairs but Perry guided her to a handsome wooden staircase, which was obviously for the family to use.

'We shall come down by the main stairs, sweetheart, but better to slip in unnoticed whilst we are so dishevelled.' He put his arm around her waist and she was somewhat reassured by the connection.

'I thought we were to be living in a separate wing?'

'We are, but obviously that has not been reno-
vated to suit us as nobody knew I would be coming
back with a bride – in fact – the family had been told I
was probably dead.'

'So where are we going to be living? In a guest
apartment?'

'No, of course not. You will have a set of rooms ad-
jacent to mine on the family side of the house.'

Her heart sank at his words. They were not to
share, but to live separately. It could not have been
made clearer that she was an unwanted extra in this
toplofty family.

'At what time do I have to come down?'

'We are not eating downstairs. I shall go and see
my brother. You must have a tray in your sitting
room.'

She blinked back her tears at his rejection and
shrugged off his arm. She entered the chambers she
had been allocated without further comment. She
was hoping he would follow her, would call her back,
but he strode off and she heard the door shut on his
own apartment.

Polly, her new maid, was yet to arrive, but a
pleasant girl was waiting to attend to her. A hip bath
had been filled and was sitting on the floor behind a

pretty lacquered screen in the substantial dressing room.

'I shall put on my nightgown and robe. I'm not going down again today.'

'Very well, my lady.'

After her ablutions were completed, her hair brushed thoroughly and plaited, she wandered into the bedchamber. The first thing she noticed was that there was no communicating door. If Perry wished to come to her he would have to walk along the main corridor.

Her bed was large and comfortable; the furnishings were modern and the decoration recent. The sitting room was equally well appointed – there was even a bookcase crammed with the latest novels. She wandered to the window and gazed out. Stretching in front of her were acres and acres of parkland. Deer grazed amongst sheep, obviously there to keep it looking tidy.

She hoped somewhere there were flowerbeds, parterres, perhaps even a maze, as endless greensward was not to her liking. From this side of the massive building, one could not see a lake; that is if they had one.

'I have changed my mind. Put out a promenade

gown and a suitable spencer and bonnet. I intend to go for a walk. I have been cooped up for too long in the carriage. Do you wish to accompany me?'

'No, my lady, I have far too much to do.'

Once dressed, Sofia took the back staircase again as she knew it led to the rear of the building. She was less likely to be seen if she remained on this side. Then she straightened her shoulders and marched down the side and eventually around the corner and onto the terrace that ran the entire width of the court.

Immediately her spirits lifted as she could see there were indeed rose gardens, pretty walks and in the distance a magnificent lake and a maze. Exactly what she wanted to explore. She set off briskly. The grass was dry underfoot, but the sun gave little warmth, unlike it did in Spain. Zorro was at her side almost immediately and she enjoyed his company. He was a connection to her previous life.

The roses were all but over, but there were still plenty of blooms there to stop and sniff. The intricate arrangements of box hedges and flower beds was interesting but what really intrigued her was the maze. She had never been inside one and was determined to do so right now.

The sun was low on the horizon. It would be dark

soon so she had better hurry, as she had no wish to be outside then. The hedges that made up the maze were at head height. When she was inside she would not be able to see over the top.

There was a container full of wooden flags. Presumably one took one in and then waved it above one's head if unable to find the way out. Excellent – this meant she could go in with impunity. She picked up one of the flags and began to explore the narrow paths. In a short space of time she arrived at the centre, where there was a pretty statue and a marble bench.

There was something in her boot and this would be an ideal place to sit and unlace it and investigate. Whilst she was so doing the sun disappeared and immediately the maze seemed less attractive, more menacing.

She was being nonsensical. Good heavens, had she not ridden out with the partisans on many occasions without being frightened? What was there to worry her about a maze?

The stone that had been annoying her was removed and she quickly did up her boot. It had belatedly occurred to her that her dinner would be arriving at any moment and she would not be there to eat it. She had no wish for a hue and cry to be set up so had better leave immediately.

'Zorro, wherever you are I need you to lead me out.'

* * *

Aubrey had been overjoyed to see him. 'I sensed something was wrong, which is why we returned to this country earlier than planned. You look remarkably well considering everything that has transpired over the past few months.'

'As do you. Married life obviously agrees with you.'

Mary had left them to talk alone, which was considerate of her. Although she was several years older than his brother one wouldn't notice the difference by looking at them. She was a beautiful young woman and obviously his twin and she were deeply in love.

'I thought perhaps you had returned because you are expecting an addition to the family.'

'No, we are not inclined to have children.' His brother grinned, making him look years younger. 'I should rephrase that: we are not unduly bothered if we do not have a family. What about you? Do you hope to set up your nursery?'

'Like you, I'm not in any hurry to share my life with screaming infants. However, I think Sofia wants a large family – so either way one of us will be pleased.'

'Well, it is not you who has to bear them for nine months and then push them out into the world. I detect a certain reservation in your voice when you talk of Sofia. Why did you marry her if you did not love her?'

Perry explained the circumstances and his brother immediately understood that he had had no choice in the matter. 'She will find it difficult adjusting to the restrictions of this life. Why don't you take the yacht and go away for a year as we did?'

'God forbid! Neither of us enjoyed the crossing from Portugal to England and vowed never to set foot on the sea again. I thank you for your kind offer, but sailing is not for us.'

The rooms that had been turned into a self-contained, and very attractive, house for his twin had been examined and admired. 'Beau said he was going to do the same for us, but until this happens we will have to remain with him. I fear he will be in no hurry to set things in motion as I think he is looking forward to having lively company for the winter.'

The door opened and Mary came in. 'I'm sorry to

intrude, but I saw Sofia go into the maze a while ago and she has yet to emerge. It will soon be too dark for her to see.'

'I thought she was going to remain in her apartment. I intended to show her everything tomorrow after we have seen the rest of the family.'

'Do you wish me to come with you, brother?'

'No, I'll find her easily enough. Forgive me, I can hardly abandon her to return here to dine with you, so I will see you tomorrow.'

He exited through the French windows and didn't bother to walk along the terrace to the central steps that led down to the lawn but vaulted over the balustrade as he had always done when a boy.

A cold wind had got up. It was like to rain and it would be decidedly unpleasant to be caught out in it. Autumn in England was quite different to this season in Spain. Here there could be frost as early as October.

He doubled across the grass, the way infantry travelled when in a hurry. His night vision had always been excellent but since his sight had returned he was finding it difficult to see clearly even when there was a full moon.

When he got within hailing distance he called

out, 'Sofia, raise the flag and then I can come in and find you.'

He was now no more than a yard or two from the entrance and expected her to reply with relief that he had come to her aid. Instead she spoke from right behind him.

'I no longer have the flag; I returned it to the receptacle. What made you think I needed your assistance in exiting the maze?'

He was not best pleased at her behaviour. 'Mary did not see you come out and was concerned for your well-being. How the devil are you out here?'

'I had Zorro. He found me a gap in the hedge to wriggle through.'

He scrutinised her more carefully and could see no evidence that she had done such a thing. There was not a single bit of greenery attached to her gown. Her bonnet, however, was askew.

'Here, let me straighten your headgear.' She remained still whilst he did so but didn't seem especially pleased by his intervention.

'I intended to dine with my brother. Why don't you come with me and meet him and my sister-in-law?'

'Was I invited?'

'You will be very welcome; you do not need a

formal invitation. He is my twin – my mirror image – he cannot wait to meet the woman I have fallen in love with.'

The tension between them lessened somewhat at his words. 'I should very much like to meet them both, but not tonight. My dinner will be arriving at any moment in my apartment and my maid will send out a search party if I am not there to eat it.'

Then she was out of his reach and running lightly across the grass without even a fond farewell. He had a deal of fence-mending to do before things were put right between them. What had upset her so much she did not even say goodbye?

Devil take it! This wouldn't do. He raced after her and caught her up easily before she reached the side entrance. He positioned himself between her and the door. The dog thought this was a grand game and barked beside them. 'Quiet, go to your bed.' He was astonished that the animal immediately was silent and loped off into the dark, leaving him to speak to Sofia in peace.

'Sweetheart, what's wrong? What have I done to hurt you so badly?'

She hesitated but then said what was in her heart. 'If you love me, why have you banished me from your bed? You could not have made it plainer that you do not wish to have me at your side by putting me in an apartment that does not connect to yours.'

'That is easily solved, my love. There are a dozen other chambers we can use. I apologise, but I did not stay long enough in my room to notice. Come, we shall find something that suits us together.'

15

What the servants would think of Perry's suggestion she had no idea, and cared less. 'I thought you had rejected me...'

His expression changed to astonishment. The next thing she knew she was in his arms and being thoroughly kissed, and her reservations about being his wife vanished under the heat of their passion.

'We cannot remain out here, darling. It is a matter of urgency that we find a suitable bedchamber.'

Instead of going in search of new accommodation they tumbled into his bed and by the time they emerged her dinner was quite cold and uneatable.

'I must eat, Perry, but it is far too late to send down to the kitchen as they will have retired long ago.'

'Then we shall go down and find ourselves something. Stay where you are, sweetheart. I'll go next door and bring you something to wear.'

'Perry,' she called urgently, 'you cannot wander about the place in your birthday suit. Put on a robe at the very least.'

'If you insist.'

He found the necessary article and then went in search of something similar for herself. She was glowing all over and no longer had doubts about her marriage. However grim – no that was doing it too brown – however difficult living at Silchester might be, as long as they shared a bed each night she would be content.

He returned and tossed her a nightgown and robe. 'These will be adequate. We are hardly likely to bump into anyone at this time of night.'

She scrambled into the garments and was about to ask where the slippers were but then decided she could manage perfectly well in bare feet this once. 'If there are eggs I can make us an omelette.'

'And I shall brew us some coffee. A feast fit for kings.'

Again, it was easier to use the secondary staircase; she was relieved that there was the occasional wall sconce still burning. 'Are these left on all night?'

'They are. It would not do for a Sheldon to be obliged to carry a candlestick about the place.'

'I wish we could live somewhere else, Perry. I don't think I shall ever be comfortable in such a grand establishment as this. Have you not a smaller estate we could remove to?'

'I have, but I wish to be close to my twin. You will soon get used to the grandeur. Anyway, next spring we shall have a separate residence and you may arrange things how you like.'

What she would like to be was away from his close-knit family where she would always be the outsider, but she could hardly tell him that. He was happy, delighted to be home and she had no intention of ruining things for him by making a fuss.

It was quite possible he was going to find it equally difficult to adjust after living such an exciting life for the past few years.

The kitchen was vast, and delightfully warm after the chilly passageway. The flagstone floor was unpleasant underfoot, but she had no option but to walk on it if she was to prepare them something to eat.

He was busy pushing and pulling levers on the giant iron range. 'There, you will have sufficient heat to do your cooking and I to make the coffee.'

She took down a flat copper pan that would be

ideal for the omelette and then went in search of the ingredients. She was no more than a few feet from her husband when he said something that made her ears burn.

'I forgot your slippers. You cannot walk about in bare feet down here.' He picked her up and placed her on the wooden chair by the long table that dominated the centre of the room. 'Sit here, sweetheart. I shall find us something to eat.' He removed the skillet from the heat – he obviously did not intend to cook anything.

Nevertheless, he found them a tasty meal of cold cuts, pickles, crusty bread and cheese followed by a hefty slice of plum cake. This was washed down with several cups of coffee. They remained in the kitchen, where it was warm, to eat it.

'That was perfect, thank you, Perry. Is there any more coffee in that pot before we go?' Suddenly the kitchen door swung open. They both turned, open-mouthed, to see the duke standing there.

'You are up late, Beau. We thought the house asleep.'

'As did I. Would you object to me joining you for your midnight feast?'

'We should be delighted. Perry is just making a fresh jug of coffee. I shall get you a plate and cutlery.'

'You will do no such thing, sweetheart. I shall do it.' Perry pointed to her lack of footwear and Beau smiled.

'In which case, Sofia, I shall collect my own utensils.' He nodded solemnly. 'An extraordinary suggestion from someone as grand as I.'

'Not half as outrageous as sleeping on the dirt as you did in Spain.'

Whilst they had more coffee Beau devoured his late supper with relish. Whilst eating he explained why he was up so late.

'Why don't I go up there in your stead?'

'I would be grateful if you would do so. Dealing with malcontents will be more your field of expertise, being a military man.'

Her pleasure in the evening was trickling away. She was to be abandoned, left to sink or swim in this draughty great house.

Then she was poked sharply in the ribs and slopped her coffee on the table. 'That was quite unnecessary, Perry. I was not sleeping, I was thinking.'

'I know exactly what you are thinking, silly girl. Did you think I would leave you behind? We might as well travel about the country until our home is ready for us.'

'I should like nothing better. I have never been to the north of England and would love to see the lakes.'

'I had hoped you would both be here for Christmas, but you could well be snowed in before your work is done, little brother.'

'If we ride we shall be there in a few days, far quicker than travelling by carriage. The luggage and servants can leave tomorrow and will be there in good time. I have no intention of departing for two days. I need to spend time with my siblings and for Sofia to get to know them before we go.' He smiled at her before continuing. 'We shall be back long before the festive period. I have no intention of celebrating anywhere but here.'

'Do you do anything special at Christmas, Beau?'

'I thought this year we must have all the family staying, children as well – not quite a house party but an intimate gathering. We have much to celebrate.'

'I have never seen a house decked out in the old-fashioned way, with ribbons and garlands and greenery everywhere. I could arrange that for you, if you would permit me?'

'Whatever you want, my dear. This is your home now. You are its chatelaine until you move into your own accommodation which won't be until next May at the earliest.'

She tried to hide her yawn behind her hand. 'If you will excuse me, gentlemen, I am weary. Please, do not get up; continue your conversation. I shall see you in the morning.'

Perry's eyes flashed. She was going to see him considerably earlier than that.

* * *

His wife was in her own bed, but Perry was content to spend the night there with her. He could hardly carry her through the corridor and back into his own domain. It was dawn when they were both ready to sleep.

'Whilst we are away, my love, we will have time to get to know each other better. I want you to be happy and will do everything in my power to make this so.'

'As long as I am with you I shall be content.' She settled into his arms and was immediately asleep.

* * *

They were woken when her maid came in and dropped the tray holding a jug of chocolate and sweet morning rolls. The crash was accompanied by a squeak of horror at finding him naked in her mistress's bed.

He started to pull back the covers.

'Don't you dare. Poor Polly has had enough shocks for one morning.'

The maid had vanished, leaving the mess on the floor. 'I shall put on my robe. I should have returned to my own chamber and not given the poor girl such a surprise.'

Sofia laughed. 'If she is to remain in my employ she will have to get used to seeing you here. Perhaps it might be wise to suggest to your valet and my maid that they wait until they are called each morning in future?'

'Excellent suggestion, sweetheart. I give you my word that by tonight we will have sleeping arrangements more suited to our wishes.'

He shrugged into his discarded robe, barely restraining himself from leaping back into bed with his darling girl, and strolled back to his chambers. After his ablutions he sat still whilst he was shaved and then dressed himself.

It would be better to go in through the sitting room door and not charge into her bedchamber. She emerged as he entered and as always when he saw her it made him catch his breath.

'Shall we go down? I hope you are not hungry as there will be no breakfast served at the usual time today – we are having an early luncheon when everyone arrives.'

'We ate a few hours ago. I wish you to run through the names of your brothers and sisters and their spouses and offspring again so that I know who is who when they come.'

'Although we have a familial resemblance, only Aubrey and I are very similar.'

'Hardly surprising, my love, when you are twins.'

The time between their rising and the arrival of the family was filled by him showing her around the house. They ended the tour and walked into the drawing room. 'Well, are you impressed?'

'Of course, but I cannot imagine why anyone would wish to build such a huge place. It can never be comfortable or warm. Even if your brother has a wife and a dozen children they will still rattle around in this massive place like beans in a sieve.'

His brother was reading a newspaper in the chamber and overheard her remark.

'I fear I shall remain a single bean in that sieve, my dear, as I have no intention of marrying.'

Any other young lady would have been disconcerted by his comment, but she smiled at him. 'Then you will be lonely, but I shall not be sorry for you, as it is your choice.' She walked across and sat gracefully on the sofa opposite and waited, tapping her foot, until he folded his newspaper and gave her his full attention.

'Thank you, your grace, I appreciate your courtesy.'

Perry had a bad feeling about this. She was about to do something outrageous and he wasn't sure if he should step in before she did or let matters unfold. He decided on the latter; no one else would take his formidable brother to task and it would do him good.

'You are a handsome man in your prime, let alone the fact that you are a duke and wealthy, and I have decided I shall not rest until I have found you a suitable wife. The Sheldons marry for love and you must do the same. Somewhere there is the perfect match for you, a young lady you will fall passionately in love with and cannot live without.'

His brother was rarely rendered speechless but on this occasion, he was. Perry waited for the icy setdown to fall upon her head. Should he step in before it happened or just pick up the pieces afterwards?

Beau, to his astonishment, laughed out loud.

'You are an original, my dear, and have said what no one else in the family has dared to. If you find me a girl I can fall in love with then I shall promptly do so. I must warn you I have had hundreds of young ladies paraded in front of me over the past years and none of them has remotely interested me.' He leaned forward to emphasise his point. 'What makes you think you can find this person?'

'I think you have been looking in the wrong places, Beau. The young ladies of the aristocracy are unlikely to be of interest to you – too insipid, too boring – I shall widen the search.'

Perry expected his brother to make it abundantly clear he would only marry a young woman from the same echelons as him. Again, he was surprised.

'You must exclude young ladies from the lower classes, naturally, but as long as the candidates are daughters of gentlemen they can be considered.'

Perry could contain himself no longer. 'This has gone on long enough, Beau. It is unkind of you to tease my wife, to raise her hopes when you intend to crush them.'

'You have misunderstood the situation, little brother. Sofia is right that I would like to be married, but I will not settle for anything less than I see between all of you.' He rose and nodded to them both. 'I have some boring estate business to attend to before the others arrive.'

Until they were alone he still expected Beau to retract his statement but he didn't. 'I cannot believe what I just heard. You have said what we have all been thinking these past few years but have not liked to say. We have discussed it amongst ourselves many times, but now we have been given permission...'

'No, my love, I have been given permission. This shall be my mission. I have not moved in such rarefied circles as all of you and am better qualified to find him a bride.'

Her calm assurance that she could do something that none of his siblings had managed irked him. She had only known Beau for a few weeks and yet believed she could find him a wife.

'We shall talk about this later. I forbid you to mention it to my family. They will be deeply offended that my wife of a few weeks believes herself better qualified than them on this subject.'

She looked away and didn't answer. His irritation turned to anger but he bit back his sharp response and strode from the room. They would discuss it later when he was calmer. Now he needed to talk to his brother and try and understand what had just been said.

Beau wasn't in the study and he was told by the butler he had gone out on estate business but would be back by eleven o'clock. Aubrey would know how to handle this – he had been married to a sensible woman for more than a year and was still blissfully happy.

He had been in parson's mousetrap for a month and was already beginning to regret his decision. Desiring his wife was one thing, but he was beginning to fear what they had wasn't real love, wasn't enough to make them both happy.

* * *

Beau surprised several lurking footmen by walking past them still smiling. Sofia was exactly what this family needed to shake it up. He had no intention of marrying, but he was going to enjoy watching her attempting to find him someone suitable. The fact that this would also keep her busy was another reason he had agreed to the preposterous scheme. Watching the expression of incredulity on Perry's face had been most enjoyable.

Without a doubt the rest of the family would wish to be involved in looking for a bride for him, and he was going to find it highly amusing observing the attempts to entice him into matrimony when he was a confirmed bachelor.

There was still an hour or two before the house would be invaded by half a dozen infants and ten adults, as well as the six who already lived here. Once they had got over the excitement of greeting their long-lost brother he would inform them that they were to stay at Silchester for the Christmas period.

He would not object if they wanted a ball at some point, possibly a supper party or two. It was probably time he mingled with his neighbours again. He would rather be on his own than spend time in the company of people he had no interest in. The fact that they lived in his vicinity was not a reason to make them bosom bows.

Sofia was right to say the house was overlarge, cold and unwelcoming. He had not thought about this before, had just accepted this was how things were, but he must give the matter some thought. Even with the two wings removed and turned into separate homes for the twins, the place was still impossibly large. He had never counted the rooms, but there must be more than a hundred.

Perhaps filling it with frills and furbelows, greenery and firs might make the place more hospitable. The custom of putting a yule log in the main fireplace in the grand hall had not been done for decades, but he rather thought he would revive this tradition as well.

He had scarcely picked up his pen when his brother marched in. With a resigned sigh he put it down and waited to see why he had been interrupted.

'What on earth made you say you would go along with Sofia's ridiculous suggestion? She is as likely to find you the young woman you wish to marry as I am to fly to the moon.' Perry straddled a chair and rested his forearms along the top. For a man supposedly in love with his wife he did not sound particularly happy.

'I shall enjoy seeing her try. I am quite aware that our siblings have been talking about doing something similar for the past year. Why are you here? It is surely not to talk about me.'

'Bringing Sofia here is like caging an exotic bird. I should have remained in Spain where she could live a freer life, not brought her back here to be constrained and bound by antiquated rules.'

'Are you saying that you are going to return there in order to keep your wife content?' His brother didn't answer. 'If she was Spanish I might have more sympathy with your concerns. However, she spent her formative years in England in a more restricted environment than this. If she genuinely loves you then she will wish to do whatever makes you happy.'

'Half the time I have no idea what she is thinking. I scarcely know her, but I do love her. I am at a loss to know what to do, what will be best for both of us.'

'Do you love her sufficiently to let her go – to open this metaphorical cage?'

'If she is already carrying our child then she must stay.' He rubbed his eyes. 'I had decided to stay out of her bed, to wait and see if she got her courses and then give her the option to leave but... well, I do not have the willpower.'

'But you do have the means. You told her you were not leaving until the day after tomorrow. Go immediately after the family have visited. Spend three weeks away and then you will know either way and can make your decision.'

'She will never forgive me for deceiving her. The last place she wishes to be is here.'

'If by so doing she gains her freedom then she will understand why you did it.'

His brother stood up. He looked haggard, the joy gone from his eyes. Whatever Perry might think to the contrary he was hopelessly in love with his wife, and losing her would destroy him.

'I shall set things in motion. Thank you for your

sound advice. It is going to be the hardest thing I've ever done. I shall pray that she is indeed with child as I don't think I could live without her now.' He rubbed his eyes again and Beau wondered if they were giving him trouble. It was only a few weeks since he had regained his sight.

'I think you must go to London and see an eye specialist before you head for the north.'

'Again, you are right. My vision is worsening again and I fear I might be going blind and this time it will be permanent.' Instead of looking desperate at the thought, Perry smiled. 'She will never leave me if I am unable to see, and I have Zorro as well. I shall manage very well whatever happens.'

16

Sofia went in search of the dog. She felt closer to the place she still considered her real home when with him. He greeted her enthusiastically and she set out for a brisk walk, keeping a close eye on the drive so she could return in time to meet her new relatives.

She couldn't see the gates as they were in a dip and by the time the first carriage was visible there would be no more than a quarter of an hour to return to the house if she wished to be there to greet them. As they were coming mainly to see Perry, she hardly thought it mattered whether she was there or not.

She kept to the paths in the hope that it would keep her gown clean and so far she had been successful. 'Come along, Zorro, we shall return along the terrace. I am sure the visitors will be here very soon.'

This route took her past the recently converted wing that was now the home of Perry's twin brother and his wife. The door flew open and if she hadn't known she would have thought it was her husband standing there.

'Sofia, what a magnificent dog.' Aubrey smiled. 'I beg your pardon, I am Aubrey. I should have introduced myself first.'

'I'm delighted to meet you. This is Zorro. He was given to Perry when he was blind, but now he has transferred his affection to me. Do you not keep dogs here? I've yet to see any wandering about.'

'Beau is not overfond of them, but the others have several. Is your animal aggressive?'

'Not at all, although he is very protective of me. I must go. The first carriage is approaching.'

By the time she had rushed upstairs and Polly had brushed down her skirts, she was sure the first arrivals would be there. Why hadn't Perry come to fetch her? She would feel more confident with him at her side.

When she approached the large gallery she could hear laughter, the shrill sound of children in the grand hall below. She was hesitating when her husband arrived at her side.

'There you are. I just went to your room to find you.' He took her hand, led her to the balustrade, leaned over and shouted at the people below, 'Good morning, I cannot tell you how glad I am to be able to see you all.'

There was a tall, dark man very similar to Beau; he must be Bennett who had returned from London. The lovely red-headed young woman holding an infant must be his wife. A toddling child was clinging onto Bennett's leg and babbling nonsense.

'This is my wife, Sofia. I shall bring her down to meet you.'

She was hugged and kissed and welcomed into the family with as much affection as she could have wished. Before they moved to the drawing room the remainder of the family, and their children, trooped in.

Eventually things were a little calmer and she was able to sit quietly with a sleeping child in her lap and observe without being obliged to participate. She recalled that Perry had said he came from a family of attractive individuals and he had not been exaggerating.

Beau joined her on the sofa. 'We are an exhausting lot when altogether. I do not blame you for taking a break from us.'

'It is Perry they have come to see. I am just...'

'You are just what?' The duke was looking at her seriously.

'I was going to say that I am just an unfortunate extra.'

'You are neither of those things, my dear. You are one of the family, as important a member as anyone else. Are you not happy to be Perry's wife?'

'I love him, but I'm not sure that will be enough. I can never be the sort of wife he needs. I feel claustrophobic here, hemmed in, unable to behave naturally. We should never have got married.'

'My brother fell in love with you almost immediately – did you not do the same with him?'

'I should never have done so if I had known who he was.' The child began to stir, giving her an excuse to end this awkward conversation. 'Please excuse me. I must return the baby to his mama.'

* * *

The house was empty again by two o'clock and she was glad of it. She needed to get out in the fresh air, pretend she was back in Spain, and gallop around the countryside. There must be a suitable mount in the stables she could take.

Polly was elsewhere, which was fortuitous as she had decided she would put on her breeches and ride astride. She would not be foolish enough to go out of the park, but today a side-saddle would just not do. She was about to pull them on but hesitated. She was sure that Mama had included a riding skirt, one that was divided into two. This would be a compromise and would surely not offend anyone.

There was a long glass in her dressing room and she viewed herself from all sides. She was satisfied she looked perfectly respectable. The secondary stairs were closer and meant she was unlikely to be seen by her husband or her brother-in-law who must be downstairs somewhere.

After the flurry of visitors, the house was quiet and had resumed its gloomy feel. The stables were empty of grooms, which was odd. She must suppose that they were allowed a short break mid-afternoon. This meant she had the pick of the horses.

As always Zorro was beside her and Billy's large head appeared and he whickered a greeting. 'I shall take you. There can be no objection to that as you belong to Perry.'

His saddle and bridle were hanging neatly on the

pegs outside his stall, and he made no objection to her tacking him up. There was an entrance at both ends of the large building and she led him to the far end in the hope that it would emerge somewhere less public than the stable yard.

'Good, a mounting block – that will make things easier for me.' The horse flicked his ears as if listening to her nonsense. Once settled in the saddle, her feet firmly in the irons, the reins in her hands, she squeezed him gently and he moved away without hesitation.

Billy was a stallion, more than sixteen hands high, and must be considered quite unsuitable for a lady to ride. But a lady would not ride astride, which was far safer on a horse of this size. Her lips curved. She had never thought of herself as a lady, but now she was Lady Peregrine Sheldon and part of one of the most prestigious families in the country.

She had noticed on her walk that morning a wide path leading into the wood that surrounded the park. This would be ideal as it was unlikely she would be seen by anyone who happened to be looking out of the windows. Neither Perry nor Beau would be impressed by her behaviour, but if she was to be happy here she must be allowed a certain amount of freedom.

* * *

Perry had spoken to Sofia's maid first thing so the girl had been aware before his wife of the change of plans. The girl had been told not to speak of it to her mistress. His valet had packed what he would need for two nights in a saddle bag and then his man would follow in the carriage with his trunk.

Beau had wanted him to take a groom, but he had refused. He would travel more speedily on his own. If he could wander about the continent behind enemy lines then he should be safe enough in the green fields of England. He had two loaded pistols in his greatcoat pockets, so in the unlikely event of being held up by a footpad he could deal with it speedily.

Sultan was also available, but in his opinion Billy was the better horse. He looked for his wife. He was unhappy about deceiving her, but she was nowhere to be found. He left the letter he had written her on her pillow. He hoped she would understand why he had gone without her when she read it.

He was going to London first to see the eye specialist, would stay at the town house tonight and then leave for the north tomorrow. With his saddle bag over his shoulder he stepped out through the front door fully expecting his horse to be waiting for him on the turning circle.

It was not there. Mildly irritated, as he had sent word down to the stable in good time, he strode around to see what the delay was. The place was in uproar. The head groom blanched when he saw him approaching.

'My lord, Billy ain't there. His tack has gone as well.'

'There is no need to panic. I believe I know where he is. Lady Peregrine is an expert horsewoman – I rather think she has taken him out herself.'

If he had announced his wife was a devil worshipper he could not have got a more astonished response. 'I'll go after her. Saddle Sultan and be quick about it.'

Zorro was also absent. He would be at his wife's side as always. He guided Sultan through the archway and into the park and sat for a moment or two considering which would be the best way to go. His eyes narrowed and he put his hand above his eyes, hoping to be able to see better.

Where would he go if he didn't want to be seen? The woods – no doubt about it. He kicked his horse into an extended canter, the horse's hooves dislodging large divots from the immaculate lawn as he thundered across.

He kept up this rapid pace for a mile and then drew rein. He put his fingers in his mouth and whistled, something that had proved useful when he had to attract the attention of his men, and waited to see if the dog would come to his side.

He whistled a second time. Sure enough, there was the sound of undergrowth moving and then the hound arrived, long pink tongue lolling from his jaws and his tail wagging wildly.

'Good boy, well done. Now, take me to Sofia.' The dog looked at the undergrowth from which it emerged and then barked. 'I cannot go that way. You must take me along the tracks.'

The animal bounded off down the path and he followed. He wasn't worried that Sofia had come to grief; Zorro would not be so lively if that were the case. He should be furious with her but he didn't blame her one jot. She was perfectly capable of riding any horse astride, but he wished she had not taken Billy as now he would be unable to ride the horse himself until tomorrow.

His appointment with the doctor would have to be postponed – but at least he could explain to her in person why he was going on his own and she wouldn't be obliged to read it in his note. The path was wide enough to canter without danger of being swept from the saddle by an overhanging branch.

In the distance he heard the hound barking, so Sofia must be aware that he was coming. It had been some years since he had ridden this way and he had forgotten that there was a clearing where the charcoal burner, in times gone by, had his hut.

His missing horse was grazing peacefully but there was no sign of her. He dismounted and left Sultan to join his stablemate. He stood in the centre of the dell and listened. The only good thing about his weak sight was the fact that his hearing had improved dramatically.

Zorro had stopped barking. The only sounds were those one would expect to hear – nothing that would reveal the presence of his beloved. He put his fingers in his mouth and whistled. Pheasants flew squawking into the air, rodents ran in horror from the racket and the dog barked.

He half-expected her to yell back but instead there was just the faint rustling of undergrowth and then she emerged.

'You took my horse.'

'How observant of you, Perry. And you have taken

your brother's. I wonder if he will come after us whistling in such an ill-bred way.'

He held out his hand but she ignored it. He had thought her remarks humorous, but now he was beginning to think he had misjudged the matter.

'Sweetheart, what is wrong? Have I offended you in some way?'

'I apologise if I sounded less than welcoming. I am out of sorts. I had thought you were busy and would not notice Billy was missing.'

There was a log large enough to sit upon at the far side of the clearing and he nodded towards it. 'We need to talk.'

He waited until she was sitting beside him and then pulled her closer so she was within his arms. For a second she resisted but then relaxed.

'I needed my horse because I had an appointment with a physician who is knowledgeable about eye problems...'

She twisted and stared at him, her expression anxious. 'Are your eyes getting worse? You should have told me.'

'They are certainly not getting any better. I can still see perfectly well to get about the place, but only if I am looking directly ahead. Do not look so worried, darling, you know that I always intended to visit a doctor on my return.'

Her eyes narrowed. 'I thought I would go with you – why were you leaving surreptitiously?'

It was right that she should know the whole but now the time had come to explain he was unmanned. Then she twisted and scrambled onto his lap and began to kiss him. He responded for a few minutes but then gently lifted her aside before things led to their inevitable conclusion.

'I have written this to you in a letter, but I am glad that I can tell you in person what is going to happen next.' He explained and she listened in silence.

'I see. You are right to go away on your own as when we are together we would have been unable to stay away from each other. I am disappointed that you did not trust me enough to tell me yourself.' She stood up and looked at him almost as if she was assessing his worth.

'I think you and your brother have bats in your attic. Did you honestly think that I would wish to re-turn to Spain, to live as your estranged wife in strait-ened circumstances? The marriage could not be set aside as it has been consummated. Neither of us would ever be able to marry again.

'You cannot get rid of me so easily, however much

of an embarrassment I am. I am your wife. If I am with child then you must hope it will be a son as there will be no more.' She nodded and was like a stranger to him. 'I assume that you intend to take a mistress. I have no objection to that as long as you are discreet.'

Her words were like a slap across his face. Not only was she someone he did not recognise, she was someone he could not like. Was this her true character? For a second he thought he had been deceived but then enlightenment dawned.

He would play along with this if it would make things easier for her. A few weeks apart would do both of them no harm and when he returned, if she was not increasing, then he would do everything in his power to get her back into his bed. He couldn't prevent his smile. Even if she was with child he could see no reason why they should remain apart.

He was jerked back to the present by a sharp kick in the shins. Sofia was standing with her hands on her hips glaring at him like an enraged fishwife.

'I have just told you I have no wish to share your bed, intend to live at your expense a life of luxury whilst giving you nothing in return – and yet you smile?'

'I was, of course, eagerly anticipating being able to sample more interesting wares. I do beg your pardon if I gave you an erroneous impression.' He turned his back on her. 'If you are thinking of attacking me, I should reconsider, my dear.' He heard a sharp intake of breath and braced himself but she heeded his words and remained where she was.

He wanted to turn, to snatch her up and kiss her breathless, to tell her that he loved her and would never be unfaithful to her, but if he was to win her back he must remain aloof and let her come to the conclusion herself that they were meant to be together.

* * *

Sofia watched him walk away taking her heart with him. What had possessed her to say such stupid things? To behave in such a cruel and beastly way? She loved him but had driven him away. What he had intended to do was the kindest, bravest thing any man could do and she had thrown it back in his face.

Then to her horror he untethered Billy, vaulted into Sultan's saddle and cantered away, leaving her to walk home. It was no more than she deserved and she wasn't going to call him back. Fortunately, her boots were comfortable and she enjoyed walking.

'Zorro, we had better follow as I believe I heard an

ominous roll of thunder in the distance. We don't want to get soaked, now do we?'

The dog wagged his tail and pressed himself against her side. He might not understand the meaning of her words but he knew she was distressed.

They were still a mile away when the rain started and when they eventually arrived she was drenched and Zorro's coat was flat against his skin. He seemed unbothered by this, whereas she was cold and miserable.

A groom appeared. 'I'll take the dog, my lady. I'll see he's nice and dry.'

She stopped at the side door to remove her boots. When she upended them water trickled out. The door opened and she was enveloped in a large blanket.

'Oh, my lady, I have a hot bath waiting for you. You must be wet through.' Her maid was stating the obvious but she was too dispirited to respond.

An hour later she was snug in bed with hot bricks at her feet. 'I do not require anything else today. I have a headache and intend to sleep. Kindly draw the bed curtains and close the shutters before you go.'

No one came to see her, no tray of tasty morsels

was brought to her; she was left to wallow in her misery and had no one to blame but herself.

17

Perry hated leaving Sofia when they were at daggers drawn, but he had to be strong if he wanted his marriage to survive. He trusted Beau to spend time with her in his absence and for the rest of his family to rally round and make her feel she was one of them and not an outsider.

He had mentioned to her that his eyesight had not improved, but he had been economical with the truth as he had not told her he was sure it was deteriorating. He wanted her to come to him from love and not from pity. If he was honest, if he thought he was losing her, then he would use whatever he had at his disposal to convince her to stay.

He arrived in good time for his rearranged appointment and was waiting in the drawing room when the doctor was announced. The man was far younger than he'd expected, his brother's age, of medium height, sandy hair and intelligent expression.

He asked pertinent questions, listened to the replies and made notes before doing an examination. 'I need you to be in direct light, my lord, so would you bring a chair to the window?'

Perry did so willingly, as to fetch a servant would have taken so much longer. 'You must be truthful, sir; nothing less will do whatever you discover.'

He was asked to turn his eyes this way and that, look up and down, but that was all.

'Done, my lord. I can categorically assure you that you are not going blind. Your sight will not get worse but I doubt that it will improve either. You have a slight inflammation caused by possibly having sand in the eyes at some stage. I recommend that you bathe them in tepid salt water twice a day.'

Until he was given this good news Perry had not realised how worried he had been. 'Thank you, I am grateful for your knowledge and advice.'

They shook hands and the visit was completed. How could something so short and simple have made such a difference to his life? He wanted to gallop back to Silchester and share the good news with his wife first, and then his family. He would have to make do with a brief note and then he would set out on his business trip and make it as brief as was possible.

* * *

He completed the journey in three days, which had allowed Billy time to recover between each stage. He was relieved to discover there was not general unrest in the area but merely a disgruntled employee who had taken to arson for revenge after being legitimately dismissed from his position as gamekeeper.

The manor house was beyond salvation and he spent a busy few days speaking to an architect and arranging for a modern house to be built in its place. The tenants were satisfied with his offer to replace their lost possessions and pay the rent on a new property for a year.

Carstairs arrived the day after him as he had travelled by mail coach but was soon fully informed and Perry was confident Beau's man of affairs could get matters brought to their conclusion without his assistance.

'I must return to Silchester tomorrow. Is there anything else I have to sign before I go?'

'Nothing, my lord – everything is ready. Do you intend to put in tenants when the house is built?'

'Why do you ask?'

'The house that is replacing the old is larger, will have all modern conveniences and you have also asked for the gardens and park to be designed by Humphry Repton. I cannot think such luxury is necessary for a tenant.'

'You are right. I wish the house for myself. I think we will be better here where things are more relaxed. I have been assured that the house and grounds will be completed within the year. Do you agree with that assessment?'

'It depends on the weather, my lord. If there is a hard winter it would delay things. If you are prepared to employ the maximum number of labourers, tradespeople and so on I am certain the building would be weathertight by the summer. Perhaps Lady Peregrine might like to visit then and decide for herself how she wants the interior to be finished?'

'I think that an excellent notion. Make certain there is a competent foreman in charge of the building.'

Satisfied he had done all he could, he returned to the fine hostelry he was staying at. He had been away for a week. It seemed like ten times that length of time. He intended to leave first thing in the morning; this meant he would be back at Silchester on the fourth day, as long as the weather remained as mild as it had this past week.

He was eager to tell Sofia of his plans for their future. His sister, Giselle, had married Lord Rushton and moved a considerable distance away from Silchester. His twin had only recently returned from gallivanting about the world for a year or more, so no one could object to him setting up home in Derbyshire.

It was a stunning part of the country, close enough to the lakes to visit there, and he was certain his family would wish to make a prolonged stay during the summer months. He and Sofia would spend the festive season at his ancestral home, so there could be no objection to his plans from anyone.

* * *

Sofia was determined not to mope about the place whilst her husband was away. He had written her a brief note saying that the eye doctor was confident his sight would not get worse, which was a relief to everyone. She now had two letters in his handwriting and reading each in turn made him seem closer to her somehow.

When she had got up the day after their argument, if it could be called that, she had been devastated to find he had already departed. Her husband was expected to be away for three weeks. That would make it almost December, and she sincerely hoped he would not be delayed by bad weather.

She spent her days visiting with her relations and getting to know them better. She was universally welcomed, her opinion respected; they could not have done more to make her feel part of their extended family. She had yet to meet Giselle who was unable to travel as she was in an interesting condition.

Over breakfast the day after Perry had left she put a suggestion to Beau. 'I should like to travel to see Giselle and Rushton – would that be possible?'

'You cannot go alone, my dear, but I should be delighted to accompany you. I have not seen either of them since the summer. Rushton is my closest friend, you know.'

'I have made enquiries and I understand it would take two days to travel there. This means if we leave tomorrow we can be there, spend a week visiting, and then be back in good time for when Perry returns.'

'I shall set things in motion immediately. Speak to your maid. She and my valet must leave today if they are to be there before us. I shall send a letter by express to tell Rushton we are coming.'

Being a duke made everything so much easier for him, Sofia decided, as she sat in luxury on the opposite side of the family travelling carriage. Mind you, if he had been impecunious and not wealthy, even being so high in the instep could not make things happen as quickly as they did.

The weather remained clement and they made good progress. She was interested in the countryside but was not silly enough to engage her companion in trivial conversation. Beau was not the sort of gentleman who would enjoy such a pastime.

Now, if Perry was here the journey would pass so much more speedily. They would laugh and talk... Her cheeks flushed at the thought of what they had done the last time they were in this carriage. 'When is Giselle's baby due to arrive?'

'In the spring sometime, I believe. This will be my sixth niece or nephew. Which reminds me, my dear, have you had any further thoughts about finding me a bride?'

'Actually, your grace, I have.'

He raised an eyebrow and his mouth curved, but he said nothing. If she wasn't already married and hopelessly in love with his brother she would find him disturbingly attractive when he was being charming.

'Well? I am all agog.'

'My thoughts are that you have no more intention of joining in with such nonsense than I have of doing it.'

His laughter filled the carriage. 'I am relieved to hear you say so. I am happy as I am, my dear. I enjoy my own company and am free to do as I please and to be as curmudgeonly as I wish.'

She smiled sweetly at him before answering. 'Married or not, sir, you will continue to do what you want and expect everyone else to fall in with your plans. You are, after all, the Duke of Silchester.'

'I am indeed and I can tell you with all honesty that there are times when I wish I was not.'

'I am astonished to hear you say so. What is it about your life that you do not like?'

'I'm one of a handful of aristocrats holding a dukedom. We are expected to behave in a certain way; those we meet feel obligated to treat us differently. Only with my family can I let down my guard. Sometimes I am tempted to abandon my life altogether – to leave Bennett to run the family.'

She stared at him, for a moment too shocked to

speak. 'Are you saying that you wish to... intend to kill yourself?'

He reacted as if stung by a hornet. 'God's teeth! Of course not – that is a coward's way out. No, I would not do that to my family and especially not to my brother who would hate to take on the title.'

'Yet you are prepared to make his son do so?'

'*Touché*, my dear Sofia. No, I merely meant that I should like to live a simpler life somewhere I could be accepted as a gentleman, not bowed and scraped to.' He warmed to his theme. 'Any young lady I am introduced to treats me differently. Perry knows without a shadow of doubt that you love him for himself, not for his title and his wealth. If I could have the same certainty, then I might consider matrimony.'

'You could always travel the country incognito.'

'An interesting suggestion, my dear, but not one that I am about to take up. I had thought I would enjoy the excitement of travelling, of camping under the stars every night, but as you are aware I could not wait to get back to civilisation.'

'Good heavens, I was not suggesting you became a pedlar. You could be a botanist recording the flora and fauna of an area for posterity.'

He chuckled. 'That would be an excellent sugges-

tion, Sofia, were it not for the fact I have no knowledge of the subject and am an abysmal artist.'

'I shall give it some thought. There must be something you can pretend to be that would allow you to
travel in comfort.' She closed her eyes and let her
mind drift, hoping inspiration would strike. Instead
her head was filled with images of Perry and she was
determined to put matters right between them when
she returned to Silchester.

Their last conversation was engraved on her
memory. How could she have said such dreadful
things? She would get her comeuppance if he took
her at her word and instead of returning directly from
the north he went to London in search of a female
companion.

* * *

When Perry was still some distance from Silchester
he was met by Zorro, who greeted him enthusiastically, covering his breeches with more mud than they
had on them already.

'I'm pleased to see you too, my boy, but why are
you so far from home? I am astonished that you knew
I was coming – but you are a clever dog and never
cease to amaze me.'

He had been fortunate in his journey as the weather had remained dry, and he had been able to ride across country most of the way. Billy showed no signs of tiring even after travelling so far. He pushed the horse into a gallop and completed the last two miles at a rattling pace, arriving at Silchester in a flurry of gravel.

The dog had been left behind but was perfectly capable of finding his own way back and would no doubt arrive shortly. He tossed the reins to a stable boy who had heard his precipitate arrival.

'Walk him until he is cool; no water whilst he is so hot.'

He strode into the house, not expecting a rapturous welcome, but for the butler to gape at him as if he was an apparition was the outside of enough.

'As you can see I am home a week earlier than expected. Would you inform his grace and Lady Peregrine that I will join them as soon as I have removed my dirt?'

'My lord, his grace and her ladyship are not in residence. They have gone to visit Lady Giselle and are expected to return at the end of the week.'

This was disappointing news. There was no point in haranguing Peebles. He would restore his appearance and then go and visit his brother. It was his own fault; he should have told them he intended to come back early.

He sent a footman to tell Aubrey he was coming and was infuriated when the response to this message was that Aubrey and Mary were also away from home for a few days. Then his irritation turned to amusement. He was behaving like a petulant child. Everyone had expected him to be away for another week so they could hardly be blamed for not being there when he had arrived earlier.

Sofia's absence would explain why the hound had been wandering about the place. The animal must think he had been abandoned. His poor valet was now trundling back in the smaller coach that was used for this purpose, so he would have to do for himself until he returned.

Hot water came without him having to send for it. He stripped to the skin and washed the grime from the journey from his person. Instead of putting on fresh garments the threw back the covers and tumbled into bed. Exhaustion after his long ride overcame him and he slept the clock around.

He got up the next morning with his day planned. He would go and see Carshalton. He had been a career soldier until inheriting the title; he would understand how difficult it was to become a civilian.

Possibly his sister Madeline's husband would give him advice that would help him settle.

It was bad form to call before breakfast had been eaten, but the family did not stand on ceremony. His arrival was seen by a vigilant servant and a groom was waiting to take Sultan from him. The front door was opened by Madeline and she flew down the steps and into his arms.

'You must be lonely with everyone away. Come in. Grey is out on estate business but should be back by lunchtime. I am about to eat breakfast – will you join me?'

'I would be happy to. How are the babies?'

'Growing up fast. I'll take you up to the nursery after we've eaten if you would like to see them?'

After spending an exhausting hour playing with the children Perry was more cheerful, resigned to the fact that he had to fill the next seven days without the company of his wife.

'I wanted to talk to Grey, but that will have to wait until he returns. Tell me, how difficult has it been for him to adjust to living like a gentleman and not a soldier?'

'After all the excitement when we were first married and his grandmother was trying to have him assassinated, one would have thought my husband would find life dull. I think he had enough excitement to last a lifetime. Jenkins and Smith had to be promised their own accommodation in return for travelling to look for you.'

'I thought as much. I had always thought to spend my life as a soldier, rising up the ranks, and only returning to England when I was too old to serve. At no time did I intend to marry or become a civilian.'

'The fact that you could be severely injured or killed at any moment did not bother you?'

'It goes with the job. I fell in love with Sofia when I didn't know who I was, if I would ever recover my memory or my sight.'

'Are you saying that you regret your marriage?'

'No, I love her and cannot live without her. What I regret is the fact that I fell in love at all – she is unhappy here and she told me she would never have become involved with me if she had known who I was.'

'You are talking in riddles, brother. I cannot see why you cavil at this marriage. You love each other; that is all that matters and you must both adjust to your new lives. I cannot believe you are so selfish you would rather have remained lost to us.'

'Beau came to find me and he would not have given up until he had done so.' He strolled towards the fire and warmed his hands. 'Which reminds me, why did he go with Sofia? I understood from Grace that once these first few months of her pregnancy are done she would be able to travel. Therefore, they will come to Silchester for Christmas, which is only a few short weeks away.'

'If you were not there to escort her she had no option but to ask Beau to accompany her. Forgive me, the housekeeper is hovering at the door and she wishes to speak to me.'

Perry left his seat and went to stare out of the window. Grey was taking an unconscionable time to return and his main purpose had been to talk to him, although he had enjoyed talking to his sister in the meanwhile.

He wandered towards the door intending to tell his sister he was leaving but, as he approached, he heard a male voice. He paused, not wishing to intrude, and overheard something he should not have done.

'I saw Perry's horse in the stable. Is he here to see me?'

'He is. Did you know Beau had accompanied Sofia to Essex?'

'That is not good news. I think your brother is

rather taken with her and she with him. Being closeted in a carriage together for three days...'

'Are you suggesting that something improper might take place?'

'Never. Silchester would not do anything untoward. I was thinking that if Sofia is not happy she might well compare her husband with him and find Perry falls short. That would not be good for either of them.'

Perry backed away. His throat was tight. He couldn't swallow. Had it come to this? Was he going to lose his wife to his brother?

18

The few days that Sofia spent getting to know Giselle and her husband reinforced her determination to make her marriage work. She would not allow Perry to be the only one in his family to have an unhappy union. Rushton was a lot older than Giselle but he did not treat his wife like a child but as an equal. She liked that about him.

Her brother-in-law spent his days out and about with his friend, leaving her alone for a considerable amount of time as Giselle was stricken with nausea on and off all day. She didn't come down for dinner, so Sofia decided she would have a tray in her room rather than eat alone with two such formidable gentlemen. She was sure they were relieved.

This gave her far too much time to think. One of the things she dwelled on, after her beloved husband, was what Beau should do in order to escape from his duties for a few months. She no longer thought of this as a way of him finding himself a wife, but to allow him to find his own version of contentment.

The gentlemen didn't suggest she rode out with them so she went out on her own every day and enjoyed her rides. Essex was rather flat and uninteresting compared to Spain and she wished with all her heart she had been able to travel to the north of England. She had heard there were hills and mountains there, which would remind her of her previous home.

On the morning of their departure Giselle was feeling a lot better and they were in the small drawing room together waiting for the carriage to be harnessed. 'I do apologise for neglecting you so shamefully, Sofia. I am looking forward to spending time with you when we come for the Christmas period. It is a great shame that Perry didn't come this time – I am the only member of the family not to have seen him since his return.'

'Thank you for being so hospitable. I am not with child, but I hope I am able to give Perry the family he wants.'

'Do not be disappointed, Sofia; sometimes it can take several months to conceive.'

'Aubrey's wife has not done so after two years. This is no problem for them as they do not wish to have children – but we do.'

The conversation ended abruptly as they saw the vehicle pull up in the turning circle. The luggage and servants had left at dawn and would be waiting at the hostelry they intended to stay at for the night.

She embraced her sister-in-law and hurried out, not wishing to keep Beau standing about. He handed her into the carriage.

'I hope you have enjoyed your visit, my dear, but I can see you are eager to get home. Perry should be back soon after us.'

'I am so fortunate to have married into your family. I cannot imagine there is another one in the country where every member is as kind, intelligent and attractive. I shall do my best to live up to your high standards.'

'My dear girl, you are our equal on every front. My brother chose the perfect wife for him. You both indicated that you wanted to have your marriage ratified in the family chapel. I thought we could do that when the house is festively decorated and the family are all here to celebrate the Lord's birthday.'

'I should love that. I just wish my mother had been present the first time and that she was not going to miss the second ceremony.'

'Wellington has all but driven the French from Spain. I think it would be safe for her to travel. She cannot be here in time for Christmas but hopefully she will be in England when there is a christening.'

She blinked back tears. 'There will be no baby next summer.'

'Do not despair, little one; these things can take time. You will have children soon enough and then might wish your nursery was not quite so full. Your accommodation will not be ready before then, so there is no rush.'

This was a strange conversation to be having with an unmarried gentleman. She had spoken to Giselle on the subject and had been told that there was no necessity to produce a baby every year if one did not wish to do so. She had not elaborated further, but had suggested that Perry speak to Rushton when they next met.

The carriage settled into companionable silence and remained that way until they paused at an inn to rest the horses and take refreshments themselves. These were ready for them and very tasty too.

As before she dined in her room and Polly had a

truckle bed at the end of hers. Once more the servants departed whilst it was barely light so they would be home and have everything ready for their arrival.

She had something interesting to tell the duke and could not wait to be on the way so that she could speak to him without fear of being overheard.

'We should be at Silchester mid-afternoon – earlier if we do not stop too long at midday. Would you rather press on or take our time?'

'I should prefer to arrive as soon as possible. I want to look my best when Perry gets back.'

'He cares little for such things, as well you know. Did you think he would have rejected you when he recovered his sight if you had not been beautiful?'

'He knew my features were regular, that...' She stopped herself just in time from saying something most indiscreet.

The only way Perry could have known her shape was if he had placed his hands on her person in a way that would be considered quite disgraceful by his formidable brother. She ducked her head and hoped the wide brim of her chip straw bonnet would hide her blushes.

'You did not answer my question, Sofia.'

'His love is not so shallow; unlike some gentlemen, he does not prize appearance above everything else.'

'Exactly so. Therefore, you are worrying unnecessarily about your marriage. It had the most unusual beginning, but I am certain you will both adjust to your new circumstances given time.'

There had been enough talk about her marriage and now she wished to discuss her plan with him.

'You cannot paint, you have no scientific knowledge, but I recall that all your family are musical – is that correct?'

'Some of us more so than others. If I had not been born first perhaps I would have concentrated more on music and might have produced something worth listening to. Why do you ask?'

'Then you should find yourself somewhere quiet, away from the grandeur and responsibilities of Silchester, and spend a few months composing.'

His smile was sad. 'There is nothing I should like better, but I cannot abandon my post. You are not suggesting this would be an opportunity to find myself a wife?'

'I have abandoned that idea. No, I just think that now you have both Perry and Aubrey to take the reins then you could be away for several months without being missed.' She knew he was going to disagree, to point out that whilst he had been in Spain things had not gone as they should because Bennett had been called to London.

'You could leave in the new year and return in the summer – the family could manage without you for that length of time and it would give you a new perspective on your life.'

'You are very persuasive, my dear. I shall give the matter some thought.' He stretched out his legs and closed his eyes, ending the conversation.

She was too restless to sleep, too excited at the thought that her husband would return to her in the next day or two. Her thoughtless words still separated them but she was confident she could persuade him she was contrite and that they were spoken in anger.

They were no more than an hour from their destination when the duke spoke again. 'There is a small estate in Herefordshire. It belonged to our mother. No one from the family has ever lived there. I believe Carstairs said the long-standing tenant had just passed away and he was having the place refurbished before finding someone else.'

She sat forward and, in her excitement at his words, put her hand on his arm. 'That sounds absolutely perfect. Nobody will know who you are. You can spend the time in solitude or mix with your neighbours if you so wish.'

There was a sudden thump on the roof. The carriage rocked to a standstill. Why had they stopped so suddenly?

* * *

Perry moved rapidly away from the door so Madeline and Grey would not know he had overheard their conversation. He turned with a relaxed smile when his brother-in-law came in.

'I wanted to talk to you, Grey, but it can wait. I wish to call in and see Bennett before I return home.'

'I am overseeing the repairs to a row of cottages so will not be about much during the day for the next two weeks.'

'The matter is not urgent. I will catch up with you both when Sofia returns.'

With a cheery wave he strode out and walked around to the stables to collect his horse. Sultan had not been untacked, the girths merely loosened, so it was a matter of moments to tighten them and be in the saddle.

He was consumed by an emotion he didn't recognise. His brother had no right to go away with Sofia, to encourage her to depend on him when she should be turning to her husband for advice. He recalled every word she had said to him the last time they had spoken. Did she believe it would be acceptable for her to take a lover? She had suggested that he find himself a mistress – he was damned if he would.

Beau he trusted implicitly. Sofia had changed since they were married and he didn't really know her. Had her wild years included sharing her favours? After all, she had come to him without a second's hesitation even though they were not married.

Had she been an innocent then? Everything had happened so quickly, he had not given the matter any thought. His brother would never betray him but he was certain there were gentlemen who would be only too happy to make love to his beautiful wife if they got the opportunity and she was willing.

He had been too lax with her. Allowed her to behave as if she was unmarried. By law she belonged to him and from this moment forward he intended to make damn sure she did as she was told or would suffer the consequences.

He didn't call in to see his brother. The mood he was in he would say something he would regret. No, this was something he must deal with himself, something private between him and his wife. The more time he spent on his own the more convinced he became that Sofia intended to play him false. Perhaps not immediately, but she would never have given him *carte blanche* otherwise. From now on he would keep her close, make sure she was never alone with any gentleman, even his brothers and brothers-in-law.

He spent his evenings drinking and fell into bed in an alcoholic stupor. Getting up each morning with a sore head and roiling guts did nothing for his temper.

Five days after his return, it was late afternoon when he eventually pulled himself together and went out for some fresh air. He saw at once that the carriage carrying the trunks had already arrived. Sofia and Beau could not be far behind. Zorro was prancing around the stable yard waiting for him.

'You are excited, old fellow. How do you know that your mistress is coming home today? Shall we go and meet her?' The animal barked as if agreeing with him.

This should have been a joyous occasion but his humour had worsened and the more he had drunk the more convinced he had become that his wife no longer loved him and wished to sever the connection if she could.

He kicked Billy into a gallop, ignoring the shocked expressions of the grooms. Mistreating one's horse was not something a gentleman should do. He was forced to stop to cast up his accounts, which did nothing to improve his mood.

He saw the carriage approaching along the lane and thundered towards it. He approached from the rear – the coachman would not have seen him – and hammered on the roof. The driver heaved on the reins and the carriage rocked to a halt.

The door swung open and his brother stepped out, looking none too pleased at the way the carriage had been stopped.

'What were you thinking? Is there an emergency that could not wait until I return?'

Perry leaned down from his horse, wanting to see Sofia. 'I need to speak to my wife. It is none of your damn business.'

Beau recoiled. 'You are drunk. You will speak to no one until you are sober.' He turned his back and jumped back into the carriage. The door slammed behind him and the driver snapped his whip.

Perry was left feeling foolish and this added fuel to his fury. He hurtled back over the hedges and ditches and arrived in the stable yard just as the carriage was turning onto the long, winding drive. Sofia would have to go to her rooms. He would be there waiting.

His valet and her maid were dismissed. His vision was blurred – he wasn't sure if it was a surfeit of brandy or if the doctor was wrong and he was indeed going blind again. A stiff drink was what he needed and there was a decanter in his sitting room. There was time enough to find it before the reckoning began.

The fact that he had eaten almost nothing these past few days, and drunk three bottles of brandy, not to mention the claret, had not enhanced either his constitution or his disposition.

He was no longer thinking straight, had allowed his doubts and jealousy to escalate to the point where he truly believed Sofia had tricked him into marriage, had already given her innocence to another, and had never loved him as she professed.

Hard drinking after a battle was expected of the officers – the men were given a pint of rum a day, which was why most of them had taken the king's shilling in the first place. But never in his life had he consumed alcohol during the day and he was no longer able to think coherently.

He drained a third glass and his hands stopped shaking. He returned to her bedchamber and prowled about the room until he began to feel unwell. She could not be here for another half an hour at least so he would rest on her bed until he heard her come in. No sooner had he closed his eyes than he passed out.

* * *

Sofia waited until Beau was back in his seat before speaking. 'Was Perry in his cups?'

'He was. I have no idea what has caused him to behave so badly – I suggest you keep your distance till I have had time to speak to him and I shall not do so until he has sobered up.'

'I was so looking forward to seeing him. In the few months we have been acquainted he has never drunk to excess, rarely had more than a glass of wine with his dinner and cider with his midday repast. Something dreadful must have happened. He has had bad news; I cannot think of any other reason why he should appear in such a rage as he did.'

'It is out of character. You must not fret, little one. I shall solve this conundrum and you will see it is no more than a misunderstanding of some sort.'

His words sent a shiver of apprehension through her. Up until that point it had not occurred to her his drinking and behaviour were somehow related to her. 'You think this is something to do with us?'

'I am certain of it. Did you part on bad terms?'

She explained what had taken place and the stupid things she had said. 'This is all my fault...'

'Nonsense. My brother is an adult; he is responsible for his own actions. If he was idiot enough to take what you said at face value then he has only himself to blame.' He reached across and patted her hand. 'How would you feel if he did indeed take himself a mistress?'

'I would be devastated – then I would take my revenge. This doesn't explain why he was angry. I can almost understand why he should drink to excess if he believed I had rejected him. But I cannot see why he would then be so furious with me – one would expect him to be sad if he truly loved me.'

'You are right to be concerned. As I said, this is based on a misunderstanding, which I intend to put right. I think it might be wise if you moved in with Aubrey until the matter is resolved.'

'I shall return to my apartment and arrange for Polly to transfer my necessities. I hope they don't object to me foisting myself upon them in this way.'

'Better to cause them a little inconvenience, my dear, than have something happen between you and Perry that cannot be put right.'

19

Sofia didn't think she'd ever get used to the size of this house – it took fully one-quarter of an hour to walk from the front door to her apartment. She walked into her sitting room expecting to hear Polly unpacking her clothes but the room was silent. That was odd – she would have to find what she wanted for herself.

Everything was laid out neatly in the dressing room and it took only a few moments to collect the items and put them into a large fabric bag. Then she added her slippers, nightgown and robe, plus clean undergarments and stockings. There was no necessity to take anything else as she hoped she would only be staying next door for one night. She had every faith in the duke to put matters right between her and Perry.

A slight sound startled her as she stepped into her bedchamber. She dropped the bag as her husband rolled off her bed, gripped the post to steady himself and then moved with remarkable speed to block her exit.

'Not so fast, madam, I need to speak to you.'

Her heart was hammering. She didn't dare stoop down and pick up her dropped clothes. This was a man she did not recognise – a man capable of anything – not the person she had married a few weeks ago.

She swallowed the lump in her throat, pressed her nails into her palms and the sharp pain steadied her a little. 'You are drunk, my lord, and I shall not speak to you until you are sober.'

'I want to know how many men you were intimate with before you married me? Do I not meet your high expectations in the bedroom? Is that why you no longer wish to be my wife?'

Whatever she had been expecting him to say, this was not it. Not only was he drunk, he had taken leave of his senses. Anger replaced her fear and she stepped in close to him. She gagged at the pungent smell.

'You are despicable. I am glad I am not carrying your child. There is now no reason for me to remain here and I shall return to Spain. I never wish to see you or speak to you again. You are not the man I thought you to be.'

He was gently swaying and she shoved him hard in the chest. He staggered backwards to sprawl upon the bed once more. She snatched up her bag and ran away. She was halfway across the gallery when her path was blocked by the duke.

'I take it I am too late. I beg you, ignore whatever he said; he will regret it when his head is clear.'

'*In vino veritas* – I think that means that the truth is always spoken by someone who is drunk. I can never forgive him for what he has said. With your permission, your grace, I will leave here in the morning and return to live with my mama in Spain. The marriage is over.'

'You will do no such thing, Sofia. I guarantee that you would regret it if you did. Love is not lost so easily. I gave you my word I would put things right. Will you allow me to do so?'

'I don't care what you do; he is nothing to me now. A man who calls his wife impure does not deserve to be forgiven. I asked for your permission out of courtesy. I shall leave whether you want me to or not.'

'Please, Sofia, will you agree to wait a week before you go? If by then you are still of the same mind then I shall escort you myself.'

She nodded. 'Very well, I will remain seven days. I shall not change my mind because I cannot unhear the words that were spoken. I have had my doubts about this union and they have just been confirmed by his behaviour. I wonder if it will be possible to have it put aside as it was conducted in the Popish religion and in a foreign tongue?'

'I hope it will not come to that, my dear, but again I vow that I shall find out for you if you are determined to sever the connection to my family.'

She curtsied and he bowed, then he stepped aside allowing her to pass. Word had been sent to Lord Aubrey and his wife that she was to be their uninvited guest for the next week. Their home had an imposing front door but it was quicker to go in through the French windows on the terrace.

Lady Mary – she must no longer think of them as family, but refer to them formally – attempted to embrace her but she stepped aside. Again, she curtsied. 'I apologise for intruding, my lady. I shall not be here above a week as I intend to return to Spain.'

'I see. I hope you will change your mind as we already consider you a dearly loved member of the family and you would be sorely missed. Please, come and sit down. I have had coffee and freshly baked pastries brought in for us.'

The last thing she wanted was to eat or drink anything but it would be the height of bad manners to refuse when Lady Mary was being so kind.

'Thank you, no cake, but I shall take coffee.'

They sat in silence and the coffee restored her equilibrium somewhat. Had her reaction been so extreme because she had been so eagerly awaiting his return? Perhaps she would have a pastry after all and another cup of coffee.

Half an hour went by before it occurred to her that Lord Aubrey had not put in an appearance. 'Where is your husband, my lady?'

'Aubrey has gone to find Perry. By the time he and Beau have finished with him he will regret his appalling behaviour.'

'What do they intend to do?'

'First they will sober him up and that will not be a pleasant experience. Then if they take a horsewhip to him it would be no more than he deserves.'

She surged to her feet, sending crockery and cake crumbs in all directions. She picked up her skirts, turned, and raced back the way she had come. If either of them dared to lay a finger on her husband it would be they who regretted it.

She had no objection to them putting his head in a bucket of water, but that was as much as she would allow. It was none of their business anyway. She and her disgraceful husband were quite capable of sorting out their own problems.

Sofia skidded to a halt in front of a startled footman. 'Where is my husband?'

'His grace and Lord Aubrey took him out for a bit of fresh air, my lady.'

* * *

Beau was pumping the handle of the well in the centre of the stable yard whilst Aubrey held Perry's head under the stream of icy-cold water. Brutal, but effective.

'I think he has had enough. Any more and we might drown him.'

'Perry, are you sober yet?' Beau had not finished with his brother. Once he was in his right mind he would understand the error of his ways.

'Devil take it, I'm half-drowned. Let me stand up, for God's sake.'

'Excellent, we are going for a brisk walk. I think the boathouse would be ideal, Aubrey.'

He stepped in and gripped his brother's arm hard enough to make him flinch. Perry looked from one to the other and he saw resignation and shame in Perry's face.

'I shall come without argument. I am a disgrace to my name and my regiment. If I had a pistol I would put an end to it right now.'

Before Beau could respond to this statement they were interrupted by the unexpected arrival of Perry's wife. She ran towards him and punched him hard. He staggered back clutching his injured nose and attempting to stem the copious flow of blood.

Aubrey had immediately released his hold on his brother before he too could be punched.

'How dare you both interfere in our business? Perry is my husband first and your brother second. I shall take care of things now. You are dismissed.'

Perry was looking as bemused as he was and Beau was relieved to see a flicker of amusement cross his face. Beau had never been told he was dismissed and hoped he would never be so again.

He nodded and tried to look formidable, but doubted he succeeded when holding a blood-soaked handkerchief to the end of his nose. 'You would do well to remember, madam, that you are a guest under my roof. An hour ago you were asking for my assistance...'

'No, sir, I was not. It was you who offered it.' She

turned to Perry. 'You had better get into something dry, my lord, before you catch a morbid sore throat.'

Perry reached out to take her hand but she moved away. Things were not resolved, but at least he could leave the two of them to take things forward from this point. He waited until she was level with him before speaking again.

'Exactly what did you think we intended to do to our brother?'

'Lady Mary said something about a horsewhip.'

'Did you really think we are such brutes?' She looked from one to the other of them and he saw doubt creeping in. 'We intended to explain in short and pithy sentences exactly what we thought of his behaviour. Believe me, my dear, that would be more than enough to put him straight.'

She looked towards the distant boathouse. 'Then why were you taking him there?'

'It would not do for us to be overheard by the staff when we are having a family debate.'

Perry made a sound, somewhere between a laugh and a groan. 'I shall come with you. I think it will be educational.'

'You will do no such thing, Lord Peregrine. I'm quite capable of telling you exactly what I think of your reprehensible behaviour. In fact, I rather think there is no necessity for anyone to say anything further on the subject as you are well aware of what you said and did.' Sofia curtsied to each of them as if they were strangers.

'I beg your pardon for punching you, your grace, but I believe that your nose will recover far sooner than my fist.'

Only then did he notice she was nursing her hand. She vanished as speedily as she had arrived, leaving the three of them alone.

He turned to his brother. 'Is she right, Perry? Do we have to explain it to you?'

'Sofia is usually right. I am a cretin. I am too ashamed to tell you what caused this abhorrent behaviour. However, once I am dry, I would dearly like to talk to both of you. Despite what has just happened, I fear I have destroyed my marriage.'

* * *

Perry was quite prepared to remain in his drenched garments to talk to his brothers. He deserved to suffer for behaving so badly.

'Get changed and then come to my study.'

His valet stripped him off and handed him a

towel. He was finding it difficult to coordinate. He was no longer bosky but not quite sober either. He would probably feel better if he ate something, but his stomach was turning somersaults and the thought of food nauseated him.

He cared not what he was wearing; he was eager speak to his brothers and prayed that they could come up with a solution to this catastrophe of his own making.

* * *

When he told them what he had thought, what he had overheard, if he had not been sitting he thought one or other of them would have pulled his cork.

'I have no excuse for my stupidity. I came back early, determined to put things right between us. Finding her absent made me anxious and then you know the rest. I had not thought myself a jealous man, but that is the only rational explanation. Unless my accident has addled my wits.'

There was a polite tap on the door and three footmen staggered in with laden trays. They hastily put them down on the leather-topped desk and vanished, leaving them to serve themselves.

'Coffee only for me, thank you,' he said to Aubrey who had immediately walked over to the food.

'When did you last eat, Perry?'

'I can't remember. I doubt I could keep anything down.'

'You will try.' Beau opened the window and tipped out the contents of a flower pot, slammed it shut and then handed him the receptacle. 'There, problem solved.'

After the first few bites his guts settled and he devoured everything put in front of him with relish. He washed it down with several cups of coffee and when he was done he felt almost human again. He wiped his mouth on his napkin and sat back. His brothers had not eaten. They were watching him and both looked less severe than they had earlier.

'How do I mend my fences with Sofia? First, I will tell you both what I have arranged for us.' He quickly told them about the house in Derbyshire he was having built and why he thought they would both be happier when life was less restricted by etiquette and rules.

'I think that an excellent notion, and it will go halfway to restoring your wife's good opinion of you. You would hardly have made these arrangements if you had been intending for her to leave and return to Spain.'

'I must warn you, Aubrey, that if Sofia does decide to go then I shall follow. I know it is the woman's place to live where her man wishes, but I will not lose her.'

Beau nodded. 'I would prefer you both to be living at Silchester, but as long as you are happy and together I shall be content.'

'Have either of you any suggestion as to how I should begin the process of winning her back?'

'Sofia has moved next door and I suggest that you do not approach her today. Allow her time to calm down. The fact that she rushed to your defence when she thought we were going to horsewhip you is a good sign.'

Perry smiled. 'I apologise for your nose, Beau, I...' He surged to his feet. 'Sofia damaged her hand. I must go at once and see she has not broken any bones.'

'Sit down; my wife will take care of her. Do you wish me to send word next door and see how she does?'

He subsided into the chair. 'Yes, please do that.' He closed his eyes and tried to marshal his thoughts into some sort of order. Until his accident he would have considered himself a sensible, calm, rational man and now he was behaving like a simpleton. If this is what love did to a fellow, he wished he was like his older brother: a bachelor with no one to worry about but himself and his duties as the duke.

When he opened his eyes again his brothers had gone, as had the trays. The fire had been banked up, the shutters and curtains closed – all this done whilst he had slept. He glanced at the overmantel clock and was shocked to see the time. He had been asleep for hours.

For the first time in several days his head was clear and he was thinking like a soldier. He had lost a battle but not the war and he was determined to court his wife and, however long it took, he would somehow persuade her to forgive him and take him back.

He emerged from the study to find the house quiet. Beau had obviously dined with Aubrey and Mary next door. He was *persona non grata* so would not intrude. Although he had eaten enough for three men before he fell asleep he was hungry again.

He saw a footman lurking at the other end of the passageway and snapped his fingers. 'Bring me something to eat. I shall have it here. Coffee also.'

When he had eaten he was wide awake and had no intention of retiring. There was a hunter's moon, which would make it perfectly safe to ride. He was already dressed in suitable garments for such an enterprise. All he needed was his greatcoat, gloves and muffler. There was a heavy frost tonight, but so far this winter there had been no snow.

Zorro, as always, appeared at his side when he reached the stables. The horses were all bedded down for the night, the grooms eating their supper in the servants' hall, and he had no intention of calling anyone back to do something he was perfectly capable of doing himself. Billy was as eager as him to get out in the crisp, cold night air.

He was not foolish enough to gallop, or jump hedges and ditches as he would do in daylight, but he had a most enjoyable excursion nevertheless. He heard the village clock strike midnight as he crunched back into the yard. He had walked the last mile so his horse was cool and could be put away immediately.

As he strolled back to the house he was aware there was no light glimmering through the closed shutter. God's teeth! Surely he had not been locked out of his own abode? He tried the side door and indeed it was locked. He marched around the house and was unsurprised to find everywhere firmly bolted for the night. He had not thought to inform a member of staff that he was going out and when Beau had returned from next door, he must have thought him asleep in his apartment.

Perhaps his brother was still awake. He often remained downstairs into the small hours reading whatever geographical journal had arrived that week. He made his way to Aubrey's wing but again it was evident no one was up.

This left him two options. He could either hammer on the door of the main part of the house in the hope that someone would hear him or spend the night in the stables. No – there was a third option. He was an agile man and he thought he might be able to climb up to the first floor and gain entry that way.

At least the moon was bright, the sky cloudless, and even with his limited vision he thought he could achieve his objective without breaking his neck. He spent a while examining the possibilities and decided to attempt to ascend to the unoccupied part of the house – the wing that his brother had intended to convert into accommodation for him and Sofia.

The shutters were not closed on the upper floors and he thought he would be able to prise up the window using the stiletto he always had secreted in his boot. He discarded his greatcoat, gloves, muffler and jacket, as it would be much easier to climb in his shirtsleeves.

There were enough protuberances for him to grasp with his fingers, but he found it difficult to lodge his toes on anything secure enough to prevent himself from falling. Slowly he moved upwards, clinging like a limpet to whatever he could find. With a sigh of relief, he reached the windowsill and heaved himself up.

He dislodged several pieces of masonry in his struggle to hold his balance and they clattered noisily to the terrace below. There was nobody sleeping in this part of the building, not even servants had their quarters in the attics, so he ignored it and slipped the blade of his knife between the window and the frame.

After several attempts the catch moved back. He got his fingers under the bottom of the window and carefully pushed it up. He swung his leg into the room and his breath hissed through his teeth. He had not realised he had been holding it.

Despite the bright moonlight outside, the interior of the room was so dark he doubted he could make his way across it without falling over something. He tried to visualise the layout, but nothing would be the same as the furniture would have been either re-moved or put in the centre and covered with cloths.

The room was colder than outside, had a damp, unused smell, and he shivered. He had a nasty feeling that having been drenched in icy water earlier, and now exposed to the elements, he was in danger of becoming unwell. The sooner he got out of this place and back into his own apartment where the fire would be lit and he could get warm again, the better.

20

Sofia politely declined to dine downstairs saying that the upset of the day had given her a megrim. 'Please, do not have a tray sent up at suppertime as I shall be asleep. Thank you for accommodating me. I gave my word to the duke that I would not leave until next week and I intend to keep my promise.'

'Your maid is now here and everything will be ready for you upstairs. Sleep well. I am sure that tomorrow things will look less painful.' Mary pointed to her bandaged hand. 'I think you have broken a bone and you should let us fetch the doctor. If it is not set it will heal incorrectly and give you pain for the rest of your life.'

'I'm sure it is nothing more than bruising, but if it

is worse tomorrow then I will see the physician.' She said goodnight and made her way to the rooms that were to be hers for the next few days.

Polly made no comment about their change of circumstances. She merely did her duty as a good servant should. Her hand was indeed extremely sore and dressing and undressing would have been impossible without assistance. Sofia dismissed the girl and said she would ring when she wanted her the next morning. Once she was alone she scrambled into bed and pulled the curtains so she was cocooned in a private space.

Running to Perry's defence had surprised her, but it had told her one thing very clearly. She was still in love with him despite his faults, and they were many, and she was no longer sure that returning to Spain was the answer. He had looked so wretched, so ashamed, and so very unwell.

The duke had explained to her why her husband had behaved so reprehensibly and she could almost understand. After all, had she not herself overreacted when she was disappointed things had not turned out the way she'd hoped? Her stomach rumbled and she wished she had not been too embarrassed to remain downstairs. Every time she looked at Beau and his swollen nose she was mortified. She had never punched anyone in her life and yet she had chosen for her first victim the formidable Duke of Silchester.

She had thought she would cry, but she was too hungry and her hand too painful for that. After tossing and turning for several hours, she abandoned the attempt to sleep and got out of bed. Her hand throbbed. Moving it was agony, and she dearly wished she had agreed for the physician to attend to her and not been so stubborn.

With some difficulty she pulled on her robe but was unable to put her injured hand through the sleeve. She needed to put her arm in a sling. She had done this for partisans who had injuries so knew exactly what to do – the problem was when she had done it for someone else she had had two good hands.

She was biting her lip and blinking back tears by the time she found a scarf she could fold into a triangle and use to support her injury. What she needed was laudanum; this was the only thing that would take away the appalling pain.

Eventually she managed to tie a knot one-handed in the scarf and then slip it over her head. As soon as she rested the damaged hand in the sling the pain eased slightly. The fire had been banked up. There was ample coal and the log basket was full. She would get it burning brightly as she thought she would be

more comfortable sitting upright on a chair than returning to bed.

Her bedchamber overlooked the terrace and she
thought she heard footsteps outside. She pulled open
the shutter and looked out of the window. Silchester
Court was built in a C-shape, the wing she was in
faced the wing the duke intended to convert for them,
as he'd done for Aubrey and Mary. To her astonishment she saw a figure climbing up the wall and then
somehow prise up the window and climb in.

Her heart almost stopped beating. Silchester was
being burgled and she must raise the alarm immediately. With some difficulty she managed to hold a candlestick in the same hand that she was using to open
the door. Mary and Aubrey had their apartment on
the other side of the wing so it did not have the same
view as her.

She knocked loudly on the door she hoped was
their sitting room. 'I have just seen a robber climb
into the house.' Her voice echoed and the door flew
open. Aubrey must have pulled on his nightshirt
hastily as it was inside out.

'Are you quite sure, Sofia?'

'Absolutely certain. The man went into an empty
bedroom in the west wing.'

Mary appeared in her robe. 'You must alert your

brother somehow. Is it possible for this villain to be able to make his way into the main part of the house from there?'

'Yes, the communicating doors are still functioning, unlike this wing.'

'Then I shall leave it to you. I bid you goodnight and I am sorry to be the bearer of such alarming tidings.'

She was about to go when Mary stopped her. 'Come in with me, my dear, and tell me how you came to be looking out of your window in the middle of the night.'

'I would prefer to go back to my room, thank you. I had just got up for a call of nature and heard footsteps outside.' This explanation appeared to satisfy and she was allowed to leave without further interrogation. The last thing that was needed at this point was for them to be worrying about her self-inflicted injury.

Now that she was out of her bedchamber she thought it might be acceptable if she went downstairs in search of something to eat. She had been given a tour of the building and was confident she could find the kitchen. The range was alight, as it should be, and it was comparatively simple to get it burning at full heat again even with only one arm –

and this her right hand, which wasn't the one she used naturally.

Mama had always said being left-handed was what had made her contrary. Most young ladies would have been forced to use their right but her parents had been more accommodating and allowed her to continue to be different. Her lips curved as she wondered if Perry had actually noticed.

The kettle was far too large for her to manage one-handed – what she needed was a small saucepan in which she could put either water or milk. Perhaps hot milk with honey would be beneficial as it should help her to sleep. This task achieved she went in search of something easy to eat with one hand. There was a large plum cake and half-eaten apple pie on one of the slate shelves in the vast larder. A piece of both of these would be ideal with her hot milk.

Taking them back to her room would be quite impossible so she dragged a chair up to the long table that dominated the kitchen and sat there. She had only ignited two candles, just sufficient for her to see what she was doing. Her hunger satisfied after devouring the cake and pie she drained her cup of milk and was ready to return. Before she could do that she must leave the kitchen in the pristine state she had found it.

Had the burglar been apprehended yet? There were dozens of male servants employed next door and she was certain they would easily overwhelm the unfortunate intruder. When the room was tidy once more she thought she would pull a chair close to the range and get warm again before venturing into the icy passageways.

Her damaged hand now hurt so badly she feared she would faint from the pain. With some difficulty she moved the rocking chair, reserved for Cook, close to the range. She rested her outstretched feet on the fender and closed her eyes, hoping that by keeping her arm still the agony would subside, thus allowing her to return to her own chamber.

* * *

Perry shuffled forward with his arms outstretched in the direction he hoped would lead him to the exit. He collided with a solid object and stumbled to his knees, cursing volubly. He fingered his way around the obstruction and then continued. Eventually his palms touched a wall – all he had to do now was sidle one way or the other and he would come to the door.

He moved right and had made the correct choice as his groping fingers touched the door frame. He found the knob and turned it. The door didn't budge. It had been locked from the outside – there was no key to turn where he was.

Once, when confined to his bedchamber for misbehaviour, he had pushed a piece of paper under the door and then managed to dislodge the key from the lock on the other side and pull it under so he could escape. He had been soundly thrashed for his disobedience but secretly thrilled he had managed to get out.

The problem at the moment was he was unlikely to find any paper in the Stygian darkness. However, he did have his knife so could attempt to dislodge the key, if indeed it was still in the keyhole on the other side, and then pray he could hook it back using the blade.

He dropped to his knees and began the delicate procedure. The key was there; he could feel it with the end of the blade. He wriggled and pushed and it fell out. Next, he lay on the floor, gripped the knife by the very end of its handle and slowly moved the blade from one side of the door to the other, praying that the key had not fallen out of his reach.

Yes – he could feel it. If he was careful he might be able to somehow wriggle it back under the door and thus be able to free himself. The alternative was climbing back the way he had come in and he doubted he was capable of doing so without falling. On his fourth attempt the key was within his finger's grasp. What he needed was something to hook it and bring it the last few inches.

His temperature was falling, and a strange lethargy was beginning to overcome him. Sitting still and going to sleep would be fatal – he had seen men perish in the bitter cold because they had refused to keep moving. He had no intention of making the same mistake. One more try and then he would wrap himself in the holland covers and march up and down the room until morning and he was rescued.

Perhaps it would be better to get his blood pumping before he had a last try. He fumbled his way into the centre of the room and for the second time almost went head first when he came in contact with the pile of furniture. The cotton sheets were voluminous and took some effort to remove. When he had folded the two he had managed to extricate, he wrapped them around his shoulders.

Then he began to walk briskly up and down the space between the window and the furniture. He did this until he was reasonably warm and then returned to the door. He flattened himself and pushed his forefinger beneath the door and just managed to hook the key.

* * *

Beau heard what Aubrey had to say with incredulity. 'Why in God's name would a burglar have chosen to climb into a disused part of the house? Good grief! The place has been empty for months. Why did they not come then?'

'You can ask him when he is captured. Now we are alerted to his presence there is no urgency as he will not get into the main part of the house without being seen. You might as well get dressed – it would not do for the Duke of Silchester to be seen in his nightshirt.'

'Do not go without me. I am quite looking forward to the experience. As far as I know there has never been a burglary here – no one before has had the temerity.'

His brother had managed to rouse the butler who had gone back to his bedchamber to dress correctly. He had been told not to bother to wake up any of the footmen as the three of them could deal with one intruder quite easily.

Aubrey was more or less dressed; there was not a

lot of difference between a white cotton nightshirt and a normal shirt in his opinion.

'Are you ready, little brother? I think we had better collect pistols from the armoury just in case he has a weapon himself.' This detour took a further fifteen minutes. Then, both of them carrying a lantern, they trekked to the far end of the house and unlocked the communicating door.

He couldn't restrain his chuckle. 'Look at that, I had forgotten I had told them to lock the rooms but leave the keys in the doors. The wretched man will not be able to get out. All we have to do is creep along the passage and listen for any movement.'

The third door they stopped at they could hear someone moving inside. Aubrey lowered the light. 'The key is on the floor. I wonder if the varmint was trying to pull it through.' He reached down and inserted it into the lock.

'Quietly now,' Beau whispered, 'try and turn it without alerting him. You get out your pistol, but put your lamp down. We will only need one – mine.'

This was done in silence. Even the key turned without a sound. He put his hand on the handle and prepared to yank the door open. He did so and they both charged forward. His feet came into contact with something solid and the next thing he knew he was spreadeagled on the floor. The lantern flew from his hand and the candle went out. The air turned blue.

'Devil take it! Aubrey, Beau, stop kicking me and let me unravel myself.'

'What the hell are you doing in here? We thought you were a burglar.'

'I went for a ride and got locked out. That doesn't explain why you two are here – how in God's name did anyone know where I was?'

Beau rolled to one side away from the melee of arms and legs and, by the faint glimmer of the lantern left on the floor outside, he could just make out Perry who appeared to be wrapped in a shroud. Aubrey scrambled to his feet and heaved his twin upright.

'It's perishing in here. Here, take my coat. Your hands are like blocks of ice.'

'No, you keep it. I shall be fully recovered once I get somewhere warmer.'

'I doubt that anywhere is particularly convivial in the middle of the night, Perry, but Peebles can rout out some help and get the fires burning in your apartment. Until then, I have no idea where we will be most comfortable.'

* * *

The three of them met the butler who was holding the greatcoat and other items he had abandoned earlier. They were too cold to be of much use to him. 'I shall be better in my bed. No need to disturb anyone. I am quite capable of making up my own fire. Goodnight and I apologise for disturbing your rest.'

Perry marched briskly up and down his sitting room to get his blood flowing freely and once he was sufficiently warm he stripped off his garments and put on his nightshirt and robe. Peebles had insisted on making up both fires and then arrived half an hour later with a tray of coffee and cake.

He drank the coffee and devoured the cake before thinking about retiring. Tomorrow he would go next door and insist on speaking to his wife. He was concerned that she might have been upset at seeing what she supposed to be a burglar climbing into the house. Then he smiled. Such a thing would be of no moment to her; she was not like any other young lady and he was glad of it.

There seemed little point in going to bed as it would be dawn soon and he intended to present himself at his brother's door before breakfast. He spent an inordinate time on his appearance and chose an elaborate knot for his neckcloth. His waistcoat was blue silk, as were the lining and collar of his coat.

Satisfied he was smart enough to plead his case, he sat at his *escritoire*, trimmed a pen and uncorked the ink. Writing down what he wanted to say to Sofia would make it easier when the time came. There might be only the one opportunity to try and persuade her to give him another chance, and he had no wish to make a sad mull of it.

After an hour the paper was still pristine. He had come up with nothing new to support his case. He could only apologise and pray she would forgive him. There was no excuse for his foolishness, unless being insanely jealous was an acceptable reason.

The clock had remained stubbornly on six o'clock and refused to move. He could wait no longer. He was going to rouse the household next door and demand to speak to his wife.

21

Sofia was woken by the startled squeal of the kitchen maid who had arrived to begin the preparations for the day. Who was the more surprised by the encounter she could not surmise. Sofia realised she had fallen asleep in the comfortable chair and spent the night in the kitchen.

'I am so sorry that I startled you. I came down for something to eat and, as you can see, I fell asleep. I shall get out of your way immediately.'

The girl curtsied. 'Never you mind, my lady, nice and warm it is in here. Shall I make you a lovely jug of chocolate and bring it up for you? I ain't supposed to go above stairs, but I don't reckon Cook will mind this once seeing as it's you.'

'That would be wonderful. I shall make sure you are not reprimanded for helping me.' Sofia was about to leave when somebody hammered on the kitchen door. She froze – memories of the burglar flooded back. Surely such a person would not bang on the door?

The maid recovered first and dashed off to investigate. To her astonishment Perry strode in and for the second time that morning she startled someone by her presence in the kitchen.

'Sweetheart, what in God's name are you doing down here?'

She was about to answer when his expression changed to one of concern and he was beside her in an instant. 'You have your arm in a sling; you are pale. Let me look at your hand.'

She flinched away. 'You must not; it is far too painful to be touched. I should have asked for the doctor to be sent for yesterday.'

Gently he pushed her back into the rocking chair and then carefully removed her injured hand from the sling. She bit back a cry of pain as he folded back the scarf to examine it. His language caused the kitchen maid to gasp.

'You have dislocated two of your knuckles. They

should have been put back in place immediately. It will be far more painful for you doing it now.'

His words had scarcely registered when he took hold of her middle fingers and held the rest of her hand steady. Then there was the searing pain and her world went black for a moment. Her scream filled the chamber.

'I'm sorry to have hurt you so badly, my love, but your hand will be better now things are back in place.'

Slowly she recovered her breath and was able to speak. She had been going to rail at him for his rough treatment but then she realised he was right. Her hand was no longer agony when she moved it. She scarcely dared to look down for fear of what she would see.

'I shall carry you back to your room, sweetheart, and then we can talk.'

Without a by your leave he picked her up and she didn't have the energy to protest. He shouldered his way through the door, past the servants' rooms and into the main part of the house.

'My room is the third door on the left, Perry.' She should have asked to be put down as she was perfectly capable of walking but being held so close to him, feeling his warmth, his strength, was exactly what she needed.

He put her into her bed and then busied himself restoring the fires before returning to her side. 'Were you up because your hand was so painful?'

'I was. Which reminds me – did Aubrey catch the burglar?'

He explained what had transpired. 'You could have been killed? What were you thinking? You might be the most aggravating of husbands, but you are the only one I have and I do not wish to lose you.'

His smile curled her toes, then she saw the familiar darkness in his eyes but he did not follow up on his desire and for that she was grateful. She was not ready to be intimate with him – there was still too much bad blood between them.

'I too could not sleep. I guessed you were having problems with your hand and wanted to see for myself what damage you had done.'

'I am so ashamed that I punched your brother unnecessarily. If my hand was so badly damaged is not his nose also broken?'

'He has a magnificent black eye but you have not marred his face.' He pulled up a chair and sat close to her, but not alarmingly so. 'I'm consumed by shame at my reprehensible and unforgivable behaviour. I have absolutely no excuse and will understand if you wish to leave me.'

'I have not quite decided what I wish to do. If the ceremony could be set aside, then we could start afresh – get to know each other better before...' She blushed, not able to mention what she had been thinking.

'I am floundering, sweetheart. You just told me you did not wish to lose me and yet you are asking to have the marriage broken. I love you, I shall never marry another, but will do whatever you want.'

'I love you too. I have not explained myself properly. I would like to be married in our own church with your family and mine present. I was just suggesting we could pretend we were courting, and then we can put everything behind us and start again.'

'We don't have to do anything about the ceremony in Spain as we can just ignore it. The family will be together here for the Christmas festivities; that will be the perfect time to have a second ceremony.' His eyes blazed and she caught her breath.

He jumped to his feet before she could respond and moved rapidly to the door. 'That being the case, my darling, I should not be in your bedchamber. I shall appear mid-morning to take you for a drive as I think that is the correct procedure for a courting couple.'

'Will I not have to remain indoors until the doctor has visited?'

'Your hand will be stiff and sore for a few days but you no longer need the attentions of a physician. I have set dislocated limbs on several occasions and he would have done nothing different.'

'I shall need bride clothes – it seems wrong to be asking you to pay for them in the circumstances.'

'Be damned to the circumstances. You order whatever you want. Will three weeks be sufficient time for you?'

'My lord, if I am to marry you a second time then I insist that you moderate your language.'

He grinned, making him look years younger. 'Coming it too brown, madam, you must have heard far worse when you were riding with the partisans.'

'I did, but somehow improper language spoken in Spanish does not sound half as bad.'

He raised a hand and disappeared. She could hear him laughing to himself outside the door. Then another voice, very similar to his, spoke.

'What the devil are you doing wandering about my house at this time of the morning?' Aubrey had been woken by Perry's laughter.

'I am going, brother. I have been speaking to my wife. She will explain it all to you at a more civilised time.'

There was a hesitant tap on her door and her brother-in-law spoke from outside. 'Are you well, Sofia?'

'I'm absolutely splendid, thank you, Aubrey. I apologise if we woke you. I shall speak to you at breakfast.'

* * *

Perry bounded down the stairs and back through the kitchen where the helpful kitchen maid was about to carry up the tray. He waved nonchalantly and left the same way he had come in. He was tempted to wake up his older brother but thought this might not be appreciated.

Zorro pressed his cold nose into his hand and whined. 'I know, your mistress is living in one place and I am in another but all will be well soon.' He patted the dog and walked around to the side door, which was now unbolted. The house was coming alive; there were several maids, sacks tied around their waists, busily scrubbing the floor. He negotiated their buckets and cloths and made his way to the study.

Peebles had anticipated his actions and the fire was lit and candles burning everywhere. He had scarcely settled in front of the fire with a newspaper when a footman arrived with a tray. Exactly what he wanted. He was drinking coffee and eating sweet rolls at exactly the same time as Sofia. They were not together in person but they were still sharing a meal.

If they were to arrange a second wedding there were invitations to send out, but perhaps it would be best in the circumstances for it to remain a family affair, as there were more than enough of them to make a jolly party. It was not the accepted behaviour to bring one's children to a house party but obviously the family would be doing so. If a larger affair was held, it meant that not only would it not be a quiet event but the guests who had been obliged to abandon their children over the festive period would be made to feel guilty.

He had left his civilian clothes here when he had bought his colours. They still fitted him well enough. It was fortunate indeed that gentlemen's fashions did not change so rapidly as those for the ladies. For their first ceremony he had worn borrowed clothes, so at least he would be wearing his own garments this time.

Beau appeared and was unsurprised to see him. 'Good morning, Perry, have you recovered from your night-time excursion?'

'Not only that, I have much to tell you, and all of it good.' He quickly ran through what had happened and what Sofia wanted.

'I think this will be a blessing rather than a marriage service, so there is no necessity to have the banns called and it can take place whenever we want. We shall use our own chapel and you are right to limit the guests to ourselves.'

'Would you object if I raided your hothouse? I wish to go laden with gifts when I visit her later.'

'I am disappointed that you feel you have to ask my permission. I am merely the custodian of all this. I do not have exclusive rights to anything.' He pointed at the empty tray, which no one had come to collect. 'Shall I delay breakfast as you have already eaten?'

'That was hours ago. I am making up now for my lack of food over the past few days. Will you come with me to choose flowers and fruit for Sofia?'

'I will not. I shall use the time to plough through the remainder of this paperwork. I am glad that Bennett was able to return from his duties in London but I believe that he has departed already and will not be back until the House of Lords rises in two weeks' time.'

'Then I shall quickly pen a note to go with what is sent. By the way, I do hope your black eye has gone before Christmas.'

His brother's smile was somewhat forced. 'As Sofia fared worse than me I am prepared to forgive and forget.'

Perry arranged to get back in time to break his fast, for a second time, and returned to his apartment to put on something against the bitter cold. Zorro followed him into the orangery and appeared intrigued by the exotic smells and bright colours. They perhaps reminded him of his former home.

He wandered about admiring the blooms and fruit but had no notion which would make the best gift.

'My lord, can I be of service to you?' The head gardener hurried up and touched his forelock.

'I need a basket of fruit and a vase of flowers to be taken to Lady Peregrine. She is visiting with Lord Aubrey at the moment.'

'Leave it to me, my lord. I will select the items myself and have them taken round as soon as they are ready.'

'They need to be there as soon as possible – before I go around myself.'

'It will be done as you requested, my lord.'

He whistled to the dog, who bounded over looking a little guilty. Perry decided not to investigate what his dog had been doing. He had a suspicion that Zorro had left a nasty surprise for one of the gardeners to find.

He wasted a further half an hour before returning to the breakfast parlour. His brother had yet to appear but the food was there and he was sharp-set. He was in the process of heaping his plate when Beau strolled in.

'You are looking more cheerful, little brother, and your colour is better too.'

'I am hopeful that in three weeks my beautiful bride will be restored to me. I shall only inform her about our future living arrangements then. I do not wish to influence her in my favour but have her take me back as I am.'

'A noble sentiment, but I do not think you can take the risk. From what you have told me she has already forgiven you – after all, she would not have suggested that you remarry if she was intending to return to Spain.'

'I shall take your advice, Beau, and tell her everything I have set in motion when I go to see her shortly. I am relieved you have not set the alterations in motion in the west wing as that would be a wasted expense. Would you ask Carstairs, when he returns, to sell the two estates I inherited. I wish to be financially independent when we move next year.'

'What do you intend to do with the money when you have it?'

'I had thought to invest in a manufactory or two – the people need work and this will be a way of satisfying my need for an income and my people for employment.'

His brother looked shocked, as well he might, because no Sheldon had ever been involved in trade before. 'I have a small interest in a shipping company. Why not investigate that first?'

'I take it that shipping is acceptable whereas manufacturing is not.' His brother frowned and Perry raised his hand to prevent the pithy retort that would be coming his way. 'As long as I don't have to sail in one myself I am quite open to putting my money in import and export instead. However, even with insurance I don't think my money will be as secure as it would be in a factory.'

'I refuse to discuss such matters when I am eating my breakfast. I had been meaning to tell you that your hound has been attracting a deal of attention in the neighbourhood.' Beau waved his fork in the air. 'Why don't you look for a suitable bitch to breed with him?'

'I rather think Zorro will find his own mate, and that there will be a surplus of puppies by next spring.'

'In which case, I shall get my kennelman to find me a couple. I have become quite attached to your dog.'

Conversation ceased whilst they both ate heartily. The time, when they had finished, was just after ten o'clock, so he must attend to his appearance and then present himself next door. This time he would go to the front as a visitor would, not to the terrace entrance.

'Are you dining next door again, Beau?'

'I thought to invite Bennett and Grace, Carshalton and Madeline, as well as Aubrey, Mary and Sofia. I think your wife will have no objection to spending time with you in company.'

'Thank you, your kindness is much appreciated. I shall see you at dinner.'

* * *

Sofia spent longer on her appearance than was strictly necessary when she was intending to spend a quiet morning in the house. Polly finished dressing her hair and stood back.

'There, my lady, that new style is perfect on you. The modiste will be arriving soon with the samples and fashion plates for you to choose your new gowns.'

'You have my measurements so there is no need for me to do more than look through the styles and materials. I'm expecting Lord Peregrine at any moment; therefore, if she arrives whilst he is here you must have her bring everything to my sitting room and I will come as soon as I can to make my selections.'

As she was admiring her appearance in the long glass there was a loud knock on the sitting room door and Polly ran to answer it. There was the sound of voices and the scuffle of feet next door and then her maid rushed in, beaming.

'This is the note that has come with the other things, my lady.'

'What other things?' She moved swiftly into the sitting room and stopped, her mouth rounded. An enormous, beribboned basket of exotic fruit stood on the central table and a huge vase of hothouse flowers had been placed on the bureau at the other side of the chamber.

She unfolded the note.

My darling Sofia,

Here are some small tokens of my love – courtesy of the duke's hothouse. I am counting the seconds until I can come and see you in person.

Love everlasting,

Your husband Peregrine

His missive was as extravagant as his gifts. She could imagine him writing it, his eyes gleaming with amusement, and loved him for it. Perhaps waiting three weeks to forgive him was a trifle longer than it need be.

22

Perry examined himself from every side and declared to his valet that he was satisfied. His measurements had been taken and they had been posted to Weston's in London where he had all his jackets made. They would make up his requirements as speedily as possible and then they would bring the almost completed articles down to him to have a final fitting.

His Hessians were so shiny they reflected the light, his neckcloth was elaborate, his shirt of the finest lawn and his jacket a deep blue that he was told matched his eye colour. He could do nothing more to impress her. His heart was skipping about as if it had become detached. He had faced a regiment of French soldiers calmer than he was feeling now.

The door opened as he approached and he was bowed in by a smart footman. 'My lord, Lady Peregrine will be happy to receive you in the yellow drawing room.'

Perry nodded and strode through the house to the smaller reception chamber that was preferred to the more formal drawing room when there was no company. The door was open and he walked in. He was not the only one who had made an effort with their dress. Sofia had on a stunning confection in pale blue with a darker blue sash and embellishments around the hem and sleeves. She had never looked more beautiful.

He had rehearsed over and over what he was going to say, how he was going to apologise again but all this was forgotten. In two steps he was beside her and she threw herself into his arms.

'I forgive you, Perry, if you will forgive me for being so silly. I agreed to marry you knowing who you were and what that would entail and I have absolutely no right to cavil now.'

'You are the most important person in my life and I will do anything to make you happy. If you want to live in Spain then that is what we shall do.'

'I will reside wherever you are – whether it's here or anywhere else. I love you and will be a better wife in future.' She smiled up at him, her eyes damp, and he was overwhelmed. Then she drew back a little. 'I said I will be a better wife but I cannot promise to be an obedient and conventional one.'

'I don't give a damn what sort of wife you intend to be, as long as you are my wife that is all that matters.'

He pulled her closer and covered her mouth with his. Only the arrival of the refreshments saved them from doing something quite outrageous.

When he told her about the house she was overjoyed. 'That is exactly what I should like. I know it is a long way from here, but we can spend Christmas at Silchester every year and your family can visit during the summer months.'

They spent a delightful two hours together until it was time for him to leave. Mary would not be able to use her sitting room until he did depart. 'Sweetheart, would you consider moving back into...'

'You will discover, my love, that Polly has already transferred my belongings. You will also see that they are in your closet as I do not intend to spend another night sleeping on my own.'

'You will have to change for dinner. Are you doing that here or next door?'

She detected his intention and smiled. 'I am not

such a pea-goose as to appear in your bedchamber before it is time to retire. I have my evening gown here. Go now, my love, and I shall see you at dinner.'

He left feeling ten feet tall. He thought he would take Zorro for a long walk and return with an hour to wait before he could change for dinner.

* * *

Beau stood up, stretched, and tossed his pen into the fire as he had done with it. Finally, the backlog of paperwork was done and he could turn his mind to family matters. He was hopeful, no, confident that Perry and Sofia would soon be back together. He would watch carefully when they were dining tonight and see how they reacted to each other.

Things were in hand for the family house party and Rushton and Giselle would be arriving next week with their daughters as they intended to stay for several weeks. He believed Giselle was finding it hard being so far from her family and he thought that she might convince Perry that moving away would be a mistake.

Of course, he had supported this notion of moving to Derbyshire; he would do anything for any of his siblings. What he would rather they did was remain at Silchester Court. If they moved to the north of England he would be lucky to see them more than once a year, especially if they started to fill their nursery.

There was an hour before he had to change for dinner. It was already dark and too late to ride, so he would find his brother and persuade him to play a game of billiards. There was something he wanted to discuss with him before he mentioned it to the others at dinner.

Perry was reading a journal in the drawing room and was only too happy to abandon it to play a frame or two. 'I have ordered two new jackets, four pairs of breeches, half a dozen shirts...'

'Enough, I have no wish to hear about such mundane things, little brother. There is something I want to talk to you about. I would value your opinion as it was Sofia's suggestion.'

'Go on, I'm intrigued.'

His brother listened with growing incredulity to the idea that the Duke of Silchester intended to remove himself from Silchester and live incognito, pretending to compose music.

'Devil take it! I thought it was I who had bats in the attic, Beau. You would hate it. You have spent your entire life being treated like a demigod, everyone bowing and scraping; being a commoner would just not suit you.'

'I was not intending to live in a hovel, Perry. The estate where I intend to live is small but profitable. I have been studying the accounts this afternoon. Elveden Hall has six bedrooms, four reception rooms and the usual servants' offices. There is also sufficient stabling for my needs and a reasonable park surrounding it.'

'You do realise, Beau, that would mean you were living in half the space that Aubrey and Mary have? A fraction of what you are used to here. I doubt it is even the most prestigious estate in the neighbourhood and you would have to allow others to have precedence when you socialised.'

'You think I could not do it for six months without scampering back here to be fêted and lauded?'

'I bet you will not last six weeks, let alone six months. Surely you are not serious with this suggestion?'

Until his brother had been so dismissive, Beau had not come to a firm decision about his venture. However, he could never resist a challenge. 'I take your wager. I shall leave when the house party breaks up. As Bennett is busy with parliamentary business I am relying on you and Aubrey to run the estate together – you will have Carstairs to assist, naturally.'

Perry slapped him on the back. 'Our house will not be finished until the summer so we must remain here anyway. Do I have your permission to move into your master suite in your absence?'

He was about to refuse but then thought better of it. 'Certainly, I wish you and Sofia to be happy here.' The sound of the gong echoed down the passageway – there was a large static one in the hall but a smaller one was always rung outside the billiard room, as they would not hear the other from here.

'At last. The afternoon has dragged by...'

'Thank you for suggesting that I am less than satisfactory as a companion, little brother,' he said with a wry smile.

His valet went about his business and Beau let his thoughts drift. If this deception was to work he would have to leave his man behind. He could not involve any of his employees. He would find himself another manservant once he was established.

In six weeks' time he would be leaving his luxurious existence for something less exalted and he was excited at the prospect. Perry knew that he was loved for himself and not his pedigree; he envied him that. Not that he was looking for love himself – far from it –

the real reason he was eager to go was to escape from the cloying atmosphere. His entire family were moon-struck with their partners and he would be glad to be away from it all for a few months.

The small estate had been well managed by the tenant, a gentleman called Richard Silverstone. It was unfortunate the man had died so suddenly, but serendipitous for him. The house was fully staffed and ready for occupation – all he had to do was send word of his coming. He would write the letter before he retired tonight.

* * *

'There, my lady, I am done.' Polly did not sound overly pleased with her efforts.

'I know wearing an evening gown to a family dinner is perhaps making me overdressed, but this ensemble has a particular significance for myself and Lord Peregrine.'

The girl dipped. 'Will you be requiring me later, my lady?'

'No, you may have the rest of the evening off. I shall ring in the morning when I require your services.'

'Thank you, my lady. Once I have tidied here, I

shall make sure that everything is ready in your apartment next door.'

Sofia had no need to pinch her cheeks or bite her lips to bring colour to them. She had never looked better. Her eyes glowed with anticipation, her hair was glossy and her gown perfect. She had intended to wear her wedding dress for the second ceremony but had changed her mind and had worn it this evening instead. This event no longer had the same significance; tonight would be the renewal of their commitment to each other.

Mary called from outside the door. 'Are you ready, my dear? Aubrey is impatient to depart as he has heard the carriages arriving. We shall wait for you by the terrace doors.'

She carefully hooked the loop of material sewn to the end of the demi-train over her wrist. She was then ready to depart. 'I'm coming. I apologise if I have kept you waiting.'

Aubrey was pacing the drawing room but his expression changed from impatient to admiration when she appeared. 'You look beautiful, Sofia. That is a particularly lovely gown.'

'Is this the one you were married in? It is quite spectacular. I am thankful that we both dressed to impress tonight or we should be put in the shade by your magnificence.' Mary gave her a brief kiss and then they dashed the short distance across the terrace and into the drawing room of Silchester Court.

They had not bothered with heavy outerwear even though the temperature had fallen and the flag-stones were frost-covered. Aubrey had no protection at all and she and Mary wore evening cloaks. The vast chamber was empty but she could hear voices in the grand hall. Perry and Beau were greeting the Shel-dons and Carshaltons.

As she hesitated Aubrey put his arm around her waist and whisked her out to join the others. Perry sensed she had arrived and turned. He abandoned his brother-in-law and strode across to her.

What he should have done is take her hand and perhaps gently press his lips to her knuckles. Instead he swept her up, crushed her close, and then his kiss was passionate and left no one in any doubt as to his views on her appearance.

'I cannot tell you how glad I am to have you back, my darling girl. You have worn that gown; it will al-ways be my favourite.'

'Perry, everyone has gone into the drawing room. We have embarrassed them by our display of... of passion.'

He chuckled and was unrepentant. 'I can assure

you, sweetheart, that all my siblings, apart from Beau, will fully understand our behaviour and even applaud it.'

'I know I am appallingly overdressed for a family dinner.'

'Come with me. I did not give you time to speak to the others.'

When he paused at the double doors she caught her breath. 'Madeline, Grace and Mary have all put on formal wear. How did they know to do so?'

The duke, resplendent in his evening black, spoke from beside them. 'Mary enquired from your maid what you were wearing and word was sent to the others. Might I be permitted to say that you look lovely.'

'Thank you. I shall never forget tonight and shall think of this as the true start of my marriage. Until today I was unsure, but now I know I made the right choice.'

Perry drew her closer so she was pressed hard against him. 'As do I. From this moment forward we shall be moving in the same direction and not pulling apart.'

After a glass of champagne Peebles announced that dinner was served. Tonight the main dining room was used despite the fact there were so few of them.

Everywhere she looked there were flowers, silverware and candles.

She scarcely noticed what she ate. The conversation sparkled, toasts were drunk and then instead of the gentlemen remaining to drink port they all moved together.

Beau remained standing and waited until they were comfortably settled. He then made an announcement that came as no surprise to her, or apparently to her husband. However, the others were astounded.

'Perry and I will be honoured to take care of things in your absence, big brother, but permit me to say that I doubt your experiment will be successful.'

Bennett looked thoughtful. 'Are we to know exactly where this estate is situated? I notice you failed to mention exactly where you would be living.'

'Carstairs is the one person who will know where I am. Only in the direst of emergencies will he contact me. Now, to demonstrate that I shall not be wasting my time, I intend to entertain on the piano for the remainder of the evening.'

If before the company had been startled, now they were dumbfounded. Perry whispered to her as the duke took his place at the keyboard. 'I have never heard him play. I am at a loss to know how he can be competent if none of us was aware of it.'

Then the room was filled with music, nothing she had heard before, but lyrical and moving. Beau played for an hour without recourse to music sheets and when the final notes died away everyone was on their feet and applauding loudly.

The remainder of the evening passed too slowly and both she and Perry were delighted when the others took their leave. She was scarcely given time to say goodnight to Beau before Perry whisked her upstairs and into his bedchamber – not his any more, but hers as well from tonight.

It didn't matter how this marriage started, what was important was how it continued and she knew without a shadow of doubt that she could not be any happier.

'I am wondering whether it's necessary to have another ceremony after all. What do you think, my love?'

'I should like to have our union blessed in our own chapel with all my family present, but I shall do whatever you want.'

She stood on tiptoe and kissed him. 'You do not have to oblige me. In future, I shall behave as I ought and be obedient to your every wish.'

His shout of laughter echoed around the chamber. 'I love you, but even I, besotted as I am, am not fool enough to believe you will be a meek and subservient wife.'

Before Sofia could disagree, Lord Peregrine tossed her onto the bed. It was fortunate that their favourite gown had been displayed for a second time, for it did not survive the night.

* * *

MORE FROM FENELLA J. MILLER

The next wonderful regency romance in The Duke's Alliance series from Fenella J. Miller, *A Duke's Bride*, is available to order now here:

www.mybook.to/DukesBrideBackAd

ABOUT THE AUTHOR

Fenella J. Miller is the bestselling writer of over eighteen historical sagas. She also has a passion for Regency romantic adventures and has published over fifty to great acclaim. Her father was a Yorkshireman and her mother the daughter of a Rajah. She lives in a small village in Essex with her British Shorthair cat.

Sign up to Fenella J. Miller's mailing list for news, competitions and updates on future books.

Visit Fenella's website: www.fenellajmiller.co.uk

Follow Fenella on social media here:

facebook.com/fenella.miller
x.com/fenellawriter

ALSO BY FENELLA J. MILLER

Goodwill House Series

The War Girls of Goodwill House

New Recruits at Goodwill House

Duty Calls at Goodwill House

The Land Girls of Goodwill House

A Wartime Reunion at Goodwill House

Wedding Bells at Goodwill House

A Christmas Baby at Goodwill House

The Army Girls Series

Army Girls Reporting For Duty

Army Girls: Heartbreak and Hope

Army Girls: Behind the Guns

Army Girls: Operation Winter Wedding

The Pilot's Girl Series

The Pilot's Girl

A Wedding for the Pilot's Girl

A Dilemma for the Pilot's Girl

A Second Chance for the Pilot's Girl

The Nightingale Family Series

A Pocketful of Pennies

A Capful of Courage

A Basket Full of Babies

A Home Full of Hope

At Pemberley Series

Return to Pemberley

Trouble at Pemberley

Scandal at Pemberley

Danger at Pemberley

Harbour House Series

Wartime Arrivals at Harbour House

Stormy Waters at Harbour House

The Duke's Alliance Series

A Suitable Bride

A Dangerous Husband

An Unconventional Bride

An Accommodating Husband

A Rebellious Bride

The Duke's Bride

Standalone Novels

The Land Girl's Secret

The Pilot's Story

You're cordially invited to

The Scandal Sheet

The home of swoon-worthy historical romance from the Regency to the Victorian era!

Warning: may contain spice 🌶

Sign up to the newsletter
https://bit.ly/thescandalsheet

Boldwood

Boldwood Books is an award-winning fiction publishing company seeking out the best stories from around the world.

Find out more at www.boldwoodbooks.com

Join our reader community for brilliant books, competitions and offers!

Follow us
@BoldwoodBooks
@TheBoldBookClub

Sign up to our weekly deals newsletter

https://bit.ly/BoldwoodBNewsletter